best sex writing
2010

best sex writing 2010

Edited by
Rachel Kramer Bussel

Copyright © 2010 by Rachel Kramer Bussel.

All rights reserved. Except for brief passages quoted in newspaper, magazine, radio, television, or online reviews, no part of this book may be reproduced in any form or by any means, electronic or mechanical, including photocopying, recording, or information storage or retrieval system, without permission in writing from the publisher.

Published in the United States.
Cleis Press Inc., P.O. Box 14697, San Francisco, California 94114.

Printed in the United States.
Cover design: Scott Idleman
Cover photograph: Plush Studios
Text design: Frank Wiedemann
Cleis logo art: Juana Alicia
10 9 8 7 6 5 4 3 2 1

Permissions appear on page 239.

Library of Congress Cataloging-in-Publication Data

Best sex writing 2010 / edited by Rachel Kramer Bussel -- 1st ed.
   p. cm.
ISBN 978-1-57344-421-7 (trade paper : alk. paper)
1. Sex--United States. I. Bussel, Rachel Kramer. II. Title: Best sex writing two thousand ten.

HQ18.U5B45 2010
306.770973--dc22
                       2009037729

CONTENTS

vii	Introduction: My Favorite Sexual Outlaws • RACHEL KRAMER BUSSEL
1	The Girl Who Only Sometimes Said No • DIANA JOSEPH
15	Secrets of the Phallus: Why Is the Penis Shaped Like That? • JESSE BERING
24	The Vagina Dialogues • JOHANNA GOHMANN
34	Sex Laws That Can Really Screw You • ELLEN FRIEDRICHS
44	What Really Turns Men On • JOHN DEVORE
49	It's a Shame About Ray • KIRK READ
60	BDSM and Playing with Race • MOLLENA WILLIAMS
79	Remembering Pubic Hair • PAUL KRASSNER
82	Sexual Outlaw • BETTY DODSON
91	Go Thin or Bust: How Berkeley's Mayer Laboratories Won the Battle of the Thin Condoms • RACHEL SWAN
104	"Sex Surrogates" Put Personal Touch on Therapy • BRIAN ALEXANDER
109	What's the Matter with Teen Sexting? • JUDITH LEVINE
114	The Anatomy of an Affair • MICHELLE PERROT
120	The Portal • JANET HARDY
124	Bite Me! (Or Don't) • CHRISTINE SEIFERT
132	Hot. Digital. Sexual. Underground. • DAVID BLACK
153	Loving Lesbians • WILLIAM GEORGIADES

- 166 Lust and Lechery in Eight Pages: The Story of the Tijuana Bibles • CHRIS HALL
- 175 The Trouble with Safe Sex • SETH MICHAEL DONSKY
- 187 Piece of Ass • MONICA SHORES
- 194 The Future of Sex Ed • VIOLET BLUE
- 203 A Cunning Linguist • JOHN THURSDAY
- 207 SWL(actating) F Seeks Sex with No Strings Attached • RACHEL SARAH
- 213 Toward a Performance Model of Sex • THOMAS MACAULAY MILLAR
- 227 The Client Voyeur • DEBAUCHETTE

- 231 About the Authors
- 237 About the Editor

Introduction: My Favorite Sexual Outlaws

If there is a theme to this year's anthology, I'd like to think it's one of being a sexual outlaw, echoing the title of Betty Dodson's essay. Because it's the outlaws who are getting the most out of sex. That's not to say that we should all be off having unconventional sex for the sake of being an outlaw, but rather that instead of listening to and blindly adhering to the conventional wisdom about sex, we need to create our own.

We see this theme in the pieces here about sex work, which defy the "sex worker as victim" trope to evoke new ideas about sex work and the people who engage in it as well as those who purchase sex. In "It's a Shame About Ray," Kirk Read is actually the one left wanting, when his client, Ray, knows exactly what he wants, and gets it. Read is left a bit wistful, wishing Ray had occupied him for a full evening rather than a mere two hours. In many ways, debauchette experiences the same thing when she's hired by a voyeur. "The intensity reminded me what it felt like to want, and not have. He hadn't touched me, but in all the silence and focused attention, I'd slowly let go of my resistance, transformed from defensive affectation to open, raw lust," she writes.

John DeVore, one of the few straight men writing a regular sex column (for TheFrisky.com), challenges his fellow males to fess up to not necessarily lusting after Megan Fox—or at least, not exclusively lusting after Megan Fox. Paul Krassner takes us back in time to an era when Brazilian bikini waxes weren't the norm, lamenting the loss of pubic hair. William Georgiades steps out of the straight male norm and into Northampton, Massachusetts, where "I soon found that the only people who were making sense to me were the die-hard gay grrrls." He navigates the tension between being a straight man, a breeder, and falling for women who sometimes, maybe, wanted him, in "Loving Lesbians," one of several essays here that defy our need to put labels neatly around sexuality. (Betty Dodson says it much more emphatically, giving herself this advice when it came to the dreaded "S/M" label: "Embrace the label to destroy its power over you.")

One of the most cherished tropes about sex is that monogamy, and marriage, are what will make us happy. That the two are intertwined is a given even in an era when BDSM and alternative sexualities are more accepted. That's why a piece like "The Anatomy of an Affair" by Michelle Perrot (a pseudonym) is so powerful. She's claiming her marriage and her sexual autonomy, stating:

> I don't want 1950s-style advice about "date nights" and lingerie and role-playing. I don't want to "spice up my marriage." I want rough sex. Dirty, spit in his mouth sex. Wet, disgusting, nasty talk about pussies

and cum and fuck-me sex. The kind of hate fucking where afterward you can't move. And the bottom line is that I don't want that kind of sex with my husband, this man I love.

Each of these authors has inspired me to think about sex in a new way, to not accept the norms, whether it's Diana Joseph defending her slutty self to both herself and her son, Judith Levine reassuring us that sexting is not the evil of teenage life it's thought to be, or Rachel Sarah weighing in on the erotic allure of breastfeeding. Noted sex and tech expert Violet Blue schools us on where our country needs to go if our sex education is truly going to serve the people it needs to, while Jesse Bering gives us a science lesson all about cock (okay, he calls it the phallus or the penis, but *cock* is my personal favorite word for that particular body part).

Some of the pieces here may unnerve you: Mollena Williams's extended meditation on "BDSM and Playing with Race" is thoughtful, honest, brave and at times, disturbing. I've included it because this is one of the most taboo topics, along with the realities of safer sex that Seth Michael Donsky uncovers. Williams calls humiliation a "delicate balancing act," and while the specific type of race-based play she's talking about takes that to an extreme, I think sex itself, and sexual fantasy, are so often very delicate balancing acts where we are trying to make sense of the insensible, or perhaps the opposite, letting ourselves lose our senses only to find something that defies logic, sense, smarts, and instead stems from the body. "For me, humiliation is a broadbrush full-bore way for me to feel the worst of how I feel about myself, give it away to someone, and have them hold it. Once someone else holds it up for me, mirrors it back, shows me the depth of my own feelings, my self-deprecation, I can see it for what it is," writes Williams.

Each of these writers brings a powerful way of looking at sex to this book. I'd love to hear what you think and welcome your suggestions for future editions of *Best Sex Writing*—feel free to contact me at rachel@bestsexwriting.com and read more about the series and my guidelines at bestsexwriting.com.

I'd also like to add that some people have commented that the erotic covers on these books trick people into thinking there will be more arousing material than what's actually inside. To me, though, as an ultimate voyeur, reading about other people's turn-ons, unearthing their sexual secrets, seeing how the other halves live, is not just educational or entertainment. It enhances my sex life because it leads me to new possibilities. These authors, the smart, daring, provocative sexual outlaws, have taught me about biology, nonmonogamy, cybersex, and so much more. I hope these essays and articles speak to your brain, as well as other organs, and at the very least, clue you in that sex is a lot bigger, broader and more complicated than you ever expected.

Rachel Kramer Bussel
New York City

The Girl Who Only Sometimes Said No
Diana Joseph

Yesterday my son was turning the pages in his eighth grade yearbook so we could play a game I came up with called Guess Which Kids Are Retarded. The boy thought the game was terrible, so cruel and so mean that I should have to pay a fine, I should have to pay him ten bucks every time I was wrong.

But I refused to pay him anything. I was horrible at guessing who was and who wasn't retarded. I've never been good at knowing something about a person just by looking at him. The ones I thought were special needs for sure turned out to be some of the coolest kids in the class, and the ones who actually were mentally retarded looked to me like members of the chess club. The problem, I decided, is most human beings between the ages of twelve and fifteen look like their needs are special. Their necks are too skinny to hold up their heads. Their teeth are shiny and enormous. There is a shifty, furtive look in their eyes, and their tongues frequently stick out at odd angles.

All the girls who I thought were sort of cute my son said yuck about. The girl he pointed out as hot did not look retarded. She looked pleased to be in front of a camera. She looked like typical cheerleader material, all blonde and blue-eyed, skinny and pretty and prissy. Then he pointed to a different girl, one in the second row from the bottom. He informed me that this girl is a slut.

"A slut?" I said. "She's thirteen years old! How can she be a slut? You don't even know what a slut is. What does that word mean to you, 'slut'? I mean, how are you defining your term? You can't just call a girl a slut and not explain what you mean by it."

The boy rolled his eyes. "What I mean," he said with exaggerated patience, "is she's been with too many guys."

"Too many guys!" I said. "Too many guys!"

The boy wanted to know why was I so worked up.

When I asked him how many guys are too many guys, he said it wasn't something that could be pinned down to a specific number. When I asked him what do you mean by "been with," what do you think "been with" implies, he said it could mean a lot of things, none of which he cared to discuss with his mother. When I asked him, well, then, how could you possibly know this girl is a slut, what evidence do you have, he said he didn't have any evidence. He said he didn't need any. He just knew.

"Right," I said. "It's one of those things a person just knows. Yes. Right. Of course. It's instinctual."

Because the boy spent most of his free time burrowed up in his room, playing endless hours of Halo, slack-jawed and mouth-breathing, pale and getting paler, hopped up on Red Bull and Oreos, pepperoni pizza and Doritos, his eyes glazed over, his breath bad, his legs atrophied from lack of use, I figured he didn't have any Biblical knowledge of this girl's sluttiness. It just wasn't possible. One would have to leave his room for that to happen. One would need to take a shower every now and then. One would have to put down his joystick.

"It's not a joystick!" he shouted. "I keep telling you that! It's a controller, okay?"

I studied the slut's yearbook picture. Long dark hair. Brown eyes. Her neck was scrawny. She was smiling and her teeth looked really big. She looked like everyone else. Unless there was someone in the know available to point it out, you'd never guess this girl was a slut. She looked like a regular thirteen-year-old girl.

Maybe it was in how she dressed. I asked the boy if this girl dressed like a slut.

"When I was her age," I told him, "I had a belt buckle that said *Boy Toy*. As soon as I walked out of the house, I went in the alley and rolled up the waistband on my skirt. I once wore my father's blue cardigan sweater to school. As a dress." I paused, raising my eyebrows so he'd understand I meant business. "It was all I wore."

The boy said what he didn't understand was why I was making such a big deal about this. "I mean, what is your problem?" he said.

"That's for me to know and you to find out," I told him. I asked my son is this girl the slut of the whole class, the slut of the whole eighth grade.

He said she was.

"Well, then," I said, "you need to know there are worse things a girl can be. She could be a person who tortures small animals, for example, or she could be someone who eats paste. She could be the girl who wears white shoes after Labor Day. White shoes after Labor Day!" I said. "That's a crime about a thousand times worse than being an eighth grade slut."

I could tell the boy wanted to argue that nobody eats paste in eighth grade, not even the retarded kids, and lots of people wear white shoes year round. He'd go on about white Reeboks, white Nikes, white Adidas—he was so predictable! But I'd already closed the yearbook. I told him Guess Which Kids Are Retarded was a terrible game, a mean game, and that I didn't want to ever hear him refer to a girl as a slut again, that girl or any other. As far as I was concerned, the matter was resolved.

"Fine," he said. "She's not a slut."

"I'm pleased to hear you say that."

The boy paused.

"She's a skanky ho bag."

In that moment, and for the rest of the day, I hated boys, just hated them.

I haven't always hated boys. There have been times when I liked them quite a bit.

I was the girl who liked boys so much that she kissed them on the first date. Sometimes I did even more. I once watched a shirtless boy, his body lean and tan, his stomach flat and muscled, his T-shirt hanging out of the back pocket of his jeans, show off for me. He did crunches while hanging upside down from the monkey bars at Lincoln Park—ninety-six, ninety-seven, ninety-eight—and when he got to one hundred, I applauded. Then I took off my shirt.

I was a girl who'd take off her shirt herself, reaching one-handed behind her back to spring open her bra. I left my footprint on the passenger's side window of a car. The guy and I got busted that night, twice, by the same cop, a bulky, jug-eared man named Officer McCormick who suggested the first time that we get on down the road. The second time he rubbed his eyes, said he had a headache, told us he had three young daughters at home who he hated to think might someday be pawed at in a car. He looked at me, sadly, it seemed, and said, "Miss, why don't you ask your gentleman friend to take you on home. It would be the honorable thing for him to do."

But the minute Officer McCormick turned his back, my gentleman friend called me Scarlett O'Hara and I called him Rhett Butler, and we giggled and talked dirty about my honor in Southern accents until one of us—okay, it was me—suggested the lake is a good place to park.

So I did slutty things. Maybe I was even sort of a slut. I probably was a slut. There were boys and other girls who thought so, said so, told each other so.

My son doesn't know this about me. He would probably be humiliated, demoralized, shocked. He'd probably consider it a form of child abuse if I ever revealed that I once had car sex with this guy on the first date, and then afterward, I opened the door and puked up a very expensive bottle of red wine. "The guy was your father, dude!" I could tell him. "What do you think of them apples?" I could say, and "Who are you calling a slut now?"

My son would be mortified, scandalized, pained to learn his mother was a girl who carried condoms in her purse or in her pocket. I kept a box of condoms in the nightstand next to my bed.

The boy doesn't know that, but he does know about condoms. When he was five years old, he walked up to me in Rite-Aid carrying a big handful, about twenty condoms individually wrapped in shiny gold foil. They kept falling out of his hands. He wanted to know what are these and what are they for.

I know he wanted them to be candy, like those chocolate coins he'd get in his Christmas stocking. "Those are condoms," I told him. "A man wears one when he doesn't want to make a baby."

"Oh, condoms," the boy said like it was a word he'd known but forgotten, like oh, of course, condoms.

"Hmmmmmp," the boy said as in I'll-be-darned and how-about-that. "Do I need one?" he wanted to know.

I told him he'd always need one. I told him sex is fun, especially when you're young and strong and healthy, and you like living in your body, but you always, always wear a condom.

"Should I put one on right now?" he said.

After I got the boy home from Rite-Aid, I gave him the big talk. I thought I did a pretty good job. I wasn't squeamish or shy or embarrassed as I told him everything I could think of concerning sex. I was frank and upfront and honest, and I did not use ridiculous words like "winky-dinky" or "willy" or "pecker" or "coochie." I called the parts of the body by their proper names, I said "penis" and "vagina," "testicles" and "secondary sex organs," I explained what various acts are and how they are performed, I talked about how some boys like girls and some boys like boys, and that's okay. "Do you think you like boys or girls?" I asked him.

"Girls stink," he said, "but I'll marry one anyway."

I showed the boy my copy of *Our Bodies, Ourselves*, I translated slang, I told him about masturbation. I wanted to cover everything.

"Hmmmmmp," the boy would occasionally say, as in that's-really-something, as in imagine-that and whodda-thunk-it.

Finally, I asked him if he had any questions.

"Can I go to the bathroom?" he said.

"Hurry!" I said. "Come right back! There's still more!"

But when half an hour passed, and he didn't come back, I went looking for him. I found him cross-legged on the floor in his bedroom, playing with Legos. He was listening to his *Barney* CD, something he hadn't done since he turned five and declared he'd had enough, he was never watching children's programming on Public Television ever again.

I asked him did he have any questions about what we'd just been talking about? Did he have any questions about sex?

He said yes.

"Ask me anything!" I said brightly. "Anything!"

He said, "What would have happened if you were a person, and Dad was an eagle, and you guys had sex, and there was an egg, a gigantic egg, and when it hatched, a baby came out, and the baby was me. Would I have a beak? Would I have talons? Would I be able to fly? It would be cool if I was half a human and half a predator bird."

"Wait right here," I told him, and I pulled my copy of *Bulfinch's Mythology* off the shelf and opened it to Leda and the Swan. While he played with Legos, I told him the story of Zeus in the form of a long-necked bird raping the beautiful Leda. I fully intended to use this as a launching point for talking about sex that's consensual and sex that's not consensual, but something in the boy's face stopped me. I think he was imagining himself emerging from a cracked egg, complete with wings, talons, a beak. I think he was imagining himself flying high above the earth, swooping down to spear a fish or a rabbit, then swooping back up to the tallest tree.

"Hmmmmmp," the boy was saying, shaking his head, as in wouldn't-that-just-take-the-cake, as in wouldn't-that-just-be-the-greatest-thing-ever.

I didn't stop talking to the boy about sex. Every so often, something would inspire me—the banana I was about to slice over his Cheerios, say, or the cigar the old man at the bus stop was chewing on, or the tubelike water balloon he was itchy to throw at me—and I'd point at the boy, I'd remind him, "You always wear a condom! Do you hear me? You always wear a condom!"

As the boy got older, he grew sick of hearing about it. "I know! I know!" he'd say. "You don't have to keep telling me that."

"You're torturing him," my friend Steven told me. "Ten years from now when he's finally having sex, he's going to hear his mother's voice in his head. And that's not something any guy wants to hear." Steven looked mournful. He was thirty-four years old and spoke to his mother every morning at seven o'clock; if he didn't call her at seven, she called him at seven oh five. Steven patted my hand, saying, "It's not good for a guy to learn about sex from his mother. Let him learn from his friends. That's how I learned, and that's where my son will learn. It really is the best way."

When my son came home from the sex ed talk he received in fifth grade, I asked him how it went. I was feeling pretty smug, pretty satisfied with my parenting skills, but the boy was furious with me. He said, "You said you told me everything! You did not tell me everything!"

Apparently, I'd neglected to tell him about his vas deferens, a part of the male anatomy I'd never given much thought. In fact, I wasn't even sure where they were or what they were for. Later that night, after the boy had gone to bed, I'd look "vas deferens" up on WebMD.com.

But right now, I was playing it cool. "Vas deferens?" I said. "Oh, yes. That's the German rock band, right?"

The boy did not find me amusing.

"A Swedish pastry chef?"

He glared, and I couldn't help myself, I said it: "Between men and women, there is a vas deferens."

The boy said if that was supposed to be a joke, he didn't get it, and I told him you will someday. I have always hated the you-will-someday response. It's another way adults can say I know something you don't know, but it's also a way adults can avoid discussing matters for which they have no answers.

It was easier to talk to my son when he was too young to do anything with the information. Now that he's older, it's more worrisome. I've been trying to think of what I could say to the boy about sex that I haven't already said. If he feels like he's justified to call a girl a slut, then I feel like I've done something wrong, like I haven't said the right thing, I haven't said enough, like I've somehow done him a wrong. I've talked plenty about penises and vaginas but maybe I haven't talked enough about the heart. Maybe I haven't said enough how easy it is to confuse love with lust, loneliness with longing. Maybe I need to say something about how important it is to be kind and careful with someone else's heart.

I was younger than my son is right now the first time I got my heart broken. I got my first kiss from Mickey Galileo who claimed he was a direct descendent of the Italian astronomer who invented the telescope and studied the stars. For a twelve-year-old's pickup line, it wasn't so bad. In fact, it must have had its charm because Mickey Galileo planted first kisses on all the girls in my neighborhood.

During our senior year of high school, Mickey would mullet his hair, and then he would perm his mullet, but now it flopped flat in a long shaggy cap over his head. I didn't like Mickey's hair, or the way he stared at my chest, or how he ran his hand up and down my back to feel if I was wearing a bra, but I did like when he pressed his chap-lipped mouth against mine, and because I liked it, I really liked it, I thought I really liked Mickey Galileo. I thought I might even love him. When Mickey told me he needed his mom's gold bracelet back because he didn't like me anymore, he was Brenda Tucci's boyfriend now, I cried. I was sad because Mickey didn't love me, but what really got me down was without Mickey, there would be no more kissing. There was no one else for me to kiss.

But then, one day after school, Nathan Evans and I stood in my backyard, and while Nella and Dutchess and Schmitty, our family mongrels, wagged their tails and watched, Nathan pushed me up against the steel gray siding of my house so he could uncurl his tongue in my mouth. Nathan was not particularly good-looking. His eyelashes and eyebrows were so pale he might as well not have had any at all. His face was long and narrow. His teeth were humongous, and his neck was skinny except for his Adam's apple.

Only I didn't care how he looked. I only cared about the kissing, how it made me feel a feeling that at the time seemed indescribable though I would now identify that feeling as horny. Very horny. I was thirteen years old.

I thought I was in love with Nathan Evans. I imagined we'd get married so we could kiss like this every day, but I'd have to adopt children since I wouldn't want any kid of mine to inherit those icky invisible eyebrows. As his mouth slurped and sucked at mine, I tried it out, those words. I murmured *I love you, Nathan Evans.* We kissed and kissed. We kissed from 3:30 to 5:00, which was when Nella and Dutchess and Schmitty started barking for their supper. Once their barking turned into howling, my mother hollered for me to feed them, and Nathan Evans, whose lips were red and puffy and swollen from all that kissing, rode away on his bike. I'd never been so happy.

Until the next day at school.

There was noise rising out of the hallways at John F. Kennedy Junior High School, and there was noise rolling out of the lunchroom and slamming off the walls in the gym, the library, my homeroom, my math class, English, Social Studies, Home Ec., and everywhere else in the school. The noise was loud and it got louder, and it all seemed to be about me. How I had sex with Nathan Evans. How I fucked him right there in my parents' backyard.

Bruce Carleton, a boy I'd known since kindergarten, licked his tongue across his lips when I passed him in the hall. Jonas Jones stuck his tongue out and wagged it at me. During lunch, Raymond Dantico kept his tongue in his mouth, but thrust it against his cheek while making throaty little moans. Billy Argot and Mark Haven and William Evans moaned and grunted while Freddie Stone asked me did it hurt.

All day that day, I kept it together. I was humiliated, I was heartbroken, but I kept my head up, I didn't cry. While I was putting forth the notion that the very idea of Nathan Evans made me want to vomit, Nathan Evans was avoiding me, going out of his way not to look at me. As far as he was concerned, his work was done. In the eyes of his peers, he'd become a man, while I became a slut. A tramp. A whore. A Girl with a Bad Reputation.

I think back to that day, and there he is, I see him, the boy. Not Nathan Evans, or Freddie Stone or Bruce Carleton, but the only boy who matters. My son. I see him wandering through the hallways of John F. Kennedy Junior High with the rest of them. He's wearing jeans and a white T-shirt and a Penn State hat even though it's against the rules to wear a baseball cap in the school. He's chewing on a toothpick. He's slouching against the lockers. He's admiring his biceps. He's as arrogant as only a thirteen-year-old boy can be. He's sure of himself and his place in the world, just as he's sure that girl walking by is a slut. Hey, he shouts at her. Hey! Did you remember to use a condom? Well? Did you?

There are still other things I could tell the boy.

At age sixteen, during the National Academic Games Championship Competition, I lost my virginity to a boy named Keith from the New Orleans team, something about that Louisiana accent, something about the way he called me honey like he was a grown man, and I was a small child. He's a doctor now.

When I was seventeen, I dated a guy named John who was majoring in chemical engineering at Youngstown State University. Every Friday night, he took me to a movie, he bought me an ice-cream cone, he made out with me in his basement, he took me home in time for my curfew. It never went any further than that. He said he respected me too much to have sex with me, though I didn't see what respect had to do with my pounding heart, my hot skin. Years later, I ran into his best friend Ed at a Rolling Stones concert. Ed informed me that after John took me home, he went to a strip club, he spent his student loan money on lap dances. John is a mailman now, and I wonder does he know that after the Stones concert, I made out with his best friend Ed, out of spite and years too late, payback for all those lap dances.

At eighteen, I was crazy about a philosophy major named Rick, who was long and lean, black-haired and green-eyed, who I let condescend to me just because I liked the way he looked. He's the unemployed father of daughters now, but back then he was so smooth.

I could tell my son that I said yes a lot, but I did sometimes say no.

I did!

I said no to a guy named Jimmy who asked me out during a parenting class. Such a class was required by the state of Colorado when a divorcing couple has a minor child. Jimmy was fat. Hairy. Wearing a thick gold chain. He wanted to know would I like to go out dancing with him after parenting class?

I said no to the boy who asked me out while standing in line at McDonald's. This was, of course, when I still ate at McDonald's, before I saw *Supersize Me*, when I was still greedy for a McDonald's cheeseburger and chocolate shake. I was twenty-eight years old, my would-be suitor was maybe sixteen.

I don't know what I said to Teddy Zeigler, a boy I knew in college. I don't know what I did with Teddy Zeigler. I don't know what happened that night except that I drank a lot, too much, I passed out, and when I woke up, blurry and stiff, sticky and fuzzy-headed, Teddy Zeigler informed me it wasn't rape, he did not rape me. "You better never say I raped you," he said, "because I didn't." Then he said here's your coat, I'll walk you to your dorm.

I try not to think about that night, what may or may not have happened.

There are still other things I could tell him, the boy, my son.

Things like:

If I had fucked Nathan Evans, then you'd have no eyebrows! The point is, if a girl's been nice enough to let you touch her boob, the respectful thing to do is keep it to yourself.

And:

Though your father and I did have sex in the car on the first date, and I did throw up afterward, he was really sweet about it, holding back my hair and offering to buy me some Seven-Up. Of course, none of this is why we got a divorce.

And:

It really is very simple. When a girl is too drunk to know she's having sex, one should not have sex with her.

And:

I liked falling in love with boys. I fell in love easily, happily, a lot. I fell in love with gay boys and bad boys, boys I'd met at the bar, frat boys and the boy my college roommate liked. From the ages of thirteen to the present, I fell in love with a redheaded paraplegic and a balding mathematician and the French student who bagged my groceries. I fell in love with a logger, a poet, a colleague. I was smitten with the doctor who delivered my son, I had a crush on an arrogant dark-haired musician with a trust fund, I was so wildly infatuated with a potter who had big hands and long fingers that in an attempt to show him how desirable and fun and sexy I was, I came on to his friend the filmmaker right in front of him. Two days later when the filmmaker invited me to go away for a weekend, I didn't go.

See? I could say. Sometimes I really did say no!

But only sometimes, the boy might point out. There were still a lot of guys. There's no denying you've been with a lot of guys.

I could ask him if he thinks "a lot" means the same as "too many." I could prepare myself for his answer. I could try to change his mind about sluts, like me, like the girl in his eighth grade yearbook, like so many girls he's yet to meet. I could tell him that he shouldn't call a girl a slut because someday she might be somebody's mother. I could tell him maybe she's a slut because she's lonely, she's sad, she's hoping someone or something will make the lonely and sad go away.

It won't, of course. It never does. But nonetheless, there's not a girl who's more hopeful than a slut, more optimistic. She may give in but she doesn't give up. She keeps looking, she keeps hoping, she's always waiting for that someone who will say it: I love you, too.

Secrets of the Phallus:
Why Is the Penis Shaped Like That?
Jesse Bering

If you've ever had a good, long look at the human phallus, whether yours or someone else's, you've probably scratched your head over such a peculiarly shaped device. Let's face it—it's not the most intuitively shaped appendage in all of evolution. But according to evolutionary psychologist Gordon Gallup of the State University of New York at Albany, the human penis is actually an impressive "tool" in the truest sense of the word, one manufactured by nature over hundreds of thousands of years of human evolution. You may be surprised to discover just how highly specialized a tool it is. Furthermore, you'd be amazed at what its appearance can tell us about the nature of our sexuality.

The curious thing about the evolution of the human penis is that, for something that differs so obviously in shape and size from that of our closest living relatives, only in the past few years have researchers begun to study it in any detail. The reason for this neglect isn't clear, though the most probable reason is because of its intrinsic snicker factor or, related to this, the likelihood of its stirring up uncomfortable puritanical sentiments. It takes a special type of psychological scientist to tell the little old lady sitting next to him on a flight to Denver that he studies how people use their penises when she asks what he does for a living. But I think labeling it as a "crude" or "disgusting" area of study reveals more about the critic than it does the researcher. And if you think there's only one way to use your penis, that it's merely an instrument of internal fertilization that doesn't require further thought, or that size doesn't matter, well, that just goes to show how much you can learn from Gallup's research findings.

Gallup's approach to studying the design of the human penis is a perfect example of "reverse-engineering" as it's used in the field of evolutionary psychology. This is a logico-deductive investigative technique for uncovering the adaptive purpose or function of existing (or "extant") physical traits, psychological processes, or cognitive biases. That is to say, if you start with what you see today—in this case, the oddly shaped penis, with its bulbous glans (the "head" in common parlance), its long, rigid shaft, and the coronal ridge that forms a sort of umbrella-lip between these two parts—and work your way backward regarding how it came to look like that, the reverse-engineer is able to posit a set of function-based hypotheses derived from evolutionary theory. In the present case, we're talking about penises, but the logic of reverse-engineering can be applied to just about anything organic, from the shape of our incisors, to the opposability of our thumbs, to the arch of our eyebrows. For the evolutionary psychologist, the pressing questions are, essentially, "Why is it like that?" and "What is that for?" The answer isn't always that it's a biological adaptation—that it solved some evolutionary problem and therefore gave our ancestors a competitive edge in terms of their reproductive success. Sometimes a trait is just a "by-product" of other adaptations. Blood isn't red, for example, because red worked better than green or yellow or blue, but only because it contains the red hemoglobin protein, which happens to be an excellent transporter of oxygen and carbon dioxide. But in the case of the human penis, it appears there's a genuine adaptive reason that it looks the way it does.

If one were to examine the penis objectively—please don't do this in a public place or without the other person's permission—and compare the shape of this organ to the same organ in other species, they'd notice the following uniquely human characteristics. First, despite variation in size between individuals, the erect human penis is especially large compared to that of other primates, measuring on average between five and six inches in length and averaging about five inches in circumference. (Often in my writing I'll relate the science at hand to my own experiences, but perhaps this particular piece is best written without my normally generous use of anecdotes.) Even the most well-endowed chimpanzee, the species that is our closest living relative, doesn't come anywhere near this. Rather, even after correcting for overall mass and body size, their penises are about half the size of human penises in both length and circumference. I'm afraid that I'm a more reliable source on this than most. Having spent the first five years of my academic life studying great ape social cognition, I've seen more simian penises than I care to mention. I once spent a summer with a 450-pound silverback gorilla that was hung like a wasp (great guy, though) and babysat a lascivious young orangutan that liked to insert his penis in just about anything with a hole, which unfortunately one day included my ear.

In addition, only our species has such a distinctive mushroom-capped glans, which is connected to the shaft by a thin tissue of frenulum (the delicate tab of skin just beneath the urethra). Chimpanzees, gorillas and orangutans have a much less extravagant phallic design, more or less all shaft. It turns out that one of the most significant features of the human penis isn't so much the glans per se, but rather the coronal ridge it forms underneath. The diameter of the glans where it meets the shaft is wider than the shaft itself. This results in the coronal ridge that runs around the circumference of the shaft—something Gallup, by using the logic of reverse-engineering, believed might be an important evolutionary clue to the origins of the strange sight of the human penis.

Now, the irony doesn't escape me. But in spite of the fact that this particular evolutionary psychologist (yours truly) is gay, for the purposes of research we must consider the evolution of the human penis in relation to the human vagina. Magnetic imaging studies of heterosexual couples having sex reveal that, during coitus, the typical penis completely expands and occupies the vaginal tract, and with full penetration can even reach the woman's cervix and lift her uterus. This combined with the fact that human ejaculate is expelled with great force and considerable distance (up to two feet if not contained), suggests that men are designed to release sperm into the uppermost portion of the vagina possible. Thus, in a theoretical paper published in the journal *Evolutionary Psychology* in 2004, Gallup and coauthor, Rebecca Burch, conjecture that, "A longer penis would not only have been an advantage for leaving semen in a less accessible part of the vagina, but by filling and expanding the vagina it also would aid and abet the displacement of semen left by other males as a means of maximizing the likelihood of paternity."

This "semen displacement theory" is the most intriguing part of Gallup's story. We may prefer to regard our species as being blissfully monogamous, but the truth is that, historically, at least some degree of fooling around has been our modus operandi for at least as long we've been on two legs. Since sperm cells can survive in a woman's cervical mucus for up to several days, this means that if she has more than one male sexual partner over this period of time, say within forty-eight hours, then the sperm of these two men are competing for reproductive access to her ovum. According to Gallup and Burch, "examples include, group sex, gang rape, promiscuity, prostitution, and resident male insistence on sex in response to suspected infidelity." The authors also cite the well-documented cases of human heteroparity, where "fraternal twins" are in fact sired by two different fathers who had sex with the mother within close succession to each other, as evidence of such sexual inclinations.

So how did natural selection equip men to solve the adaptive problem of other men impregnating their sexual partners? The answer, according to Gallup, is their penises were sculpted in such a way that the organ would effectively displace the semen of competitors from their partner's vagina, a well-synchronized effect facilitated by the "upsuck" of thrusting during intercourse. Specifically, the coronal ridge offers a special removal service by expunging foreign sperm. According to this analysis, the effect of thrusting would be to draw other men's sperm away from the cervix and back around the glans, thus "scooping out" the semen deposited by a sexual rival.

You might think that's fine and dandy, but one couldn't possibly prove such a thing. But you'd be underestimating Gallup, who in addition to being a brilliant evolutionary theorist, happens also to be a very talented experimental researcher (among other things, he's also well-known for developing the famous mirror self-recognition test for use with chimpanzees back in the early 1970s). In a series of studies published in a 2003 issue of the journal *Evolution & Human Behavior*, Gallup and a team of his students put the "semen displacement hypothesis" to the test using artificial genitalia of different shapes and sizes. They even concocted several batches of realistic seminal fluid. Findings from the study may not have "proved" the semen displacement hypothesis, but it certainly confirmed its principal points and made a believer out of most readers.

Here's how the basic study design worked. (And perhaps I ought to preempt the usual refrain by pointing out firstly that, yes, Gallup and his coauthors did receive full ethical approval from their university to conduct this study.) The researchers selected several sets of prosthetic genitals from erotic novelty stores, including a realistic latex vagina sold as a masturbation pal for lonely straight men and tied off at one end to prevent leakage, and three artificial phalluses. The first latex phallus was 6.1 inches long and 1.3 inches in diameter with a coronal ridge extending approximately 0.20 inch from the shaft. The second phallus was the same length, but its coronal ridge extended only 0.12 inch from the shaft. Finally, the third phallus matched the other two in length, but lacked a coronal ridge entirely. In other words, whereas the first two phalluses closely resembled an actual human penis, varying only in the coronal ridge properties, the third (the control phallus) was the bland and headless horseman of the bunch.

Next, the authors borrowed a recipe for simulated semen from another evolutionary psychologist, Todd Shackleford from Florida Atlantic University, and created several batches of seminal fluid. The recipe "consisted of 0.08 cups of sifted, white, unbleached flour mixed with 1.06 cups of water. This mixture was brought to a boil, simmered for 15 minutes while being stirred, and allowed to cool." In a controlled series of "displacement trials," the vagina was then loaded with semen, the phalluses were inserted at varying depths (to simulate thrusting) and removed, whereupon the latex orifice was examined to determine how much semen had been displaced from it. As predicted, the two phalluses with the coronal ridges displaced significantly more semen from the vagina (each removed 91 percent) than the "headless" control (35.3 percent). Additionally, the further that the phalluses were inserted—that is to say, the deeper the thrust—the more semen was displaced. When the phallus with the more impressive coronal ridge was inserted three fourths of the way into the vagina, it removed only a third of the semen, whereas it removed nearly all of the semen when inserted completely. Shallow thrusting, simulated by the researchers inserting the artificial phallus halfway or less into the artificial vagina, failed to displace any semen at all. So if you want advice that'll give you a leg up in the evolutionary arms race, don't go West, young man—go deep.

In the second part of their study published in *Evolution & Human Behavior,* Gallup administered a series of survey questions to college-age students about their sexual history. These questions were meant to determine whether penile behavior (my term, not theirs) could be predicted based on the men's suspicion of infidelity in their partners. In the first of these anonymous questionnaires, both men and women reported that, in the wake of allegations of female cheating, men thrust deeper and faster. Results from a second questionnaire revealed that, upon first being sexually reunited after time apart, couples engaged in more vigorous sex—namely, compared to baseline sexual activity where couples see each other more regularly, vaginal intercourse following periods of separation involves deeper and quicker thrusting. Hopefully you're thinking as an evolutionary psychologist at this point and can infer what these survey data mean: by using their penises proficiently as a semen displacement device, men are subconsciously (in some cases consciously) combating the possibility that their partners have had sex with another man in their absence. The really beautiful thing about evolutionary psychology is that you don't have to believe it's true for it to work precisely this way. Natural selection doesn't much mind if you favor an alternative explanation for why you get so randy upon being reunited with your partner. Your penis will go about its business of displacing sperm regardless.

There are many other related hypotheses that can be derived from the semen displacement theory. In their 2004 *Evolutionary Psychology* piece, for example, Gallup and Burch expound on a number of fascinating spin-off ideas. For example, one obvious criticism of the semen displacement theory is that men would essentially disadvantage their own reproductive success by removing their own sperm cells from their sexual partner. However, in your own sex life, you've probably noticed the "refractory period" immediately following ejaculation, during which males almost instantly lose their tumescence (the erection deflates to half its full size within one minute of ejaculating), their penises become rather hypersensitive and further thrusting even turns somewhat unpleasant. In fact, for anywhere between thirty minutes to twenty-four hours, men are rendered temporarily impotent following ejaculation. According to Gallup and Burch, these post-ejaculatory features, in addition to the common "sedation" effect of orgasm, may be adaptations to the problem of "self-semen displacement."

Gallup and Burch also leave us with a very intriguing hypothetical question. "Is it possible (short of artificial insemination)," they ask, "for a woman to become pregnant by a man she never had sex with? We think the answer is 'yes.'" It's a tricky run to wrap your head around, but basically Gallup and Burch say that semen displacement theory predicts that this is possible in the following way. I've taken the liberty of editing this for clarity. Also note that the scenario is especially relevant to uncircumcised men.

> If "Josh" were to have sex with "Kate" who recently had sex with "Mike," in the process of thrusting his penis back and forth in her vagina, some of Mike's semen would be forced under Josh's frenulum, collected behind his coronal ridge, and displaced from the area proximate to the cervix. After Josh ejaculates and substitutes his semen for that of the other male, as he withdraws from the vagina some of Mike's semen will still be present on the shaft of his penis and behind his coronal ridge. As his erection subsides the glans will withdraw under the foreskin, raising the possibility that some of Mike's semen could be captured underneath the foreskin and behind the coronal ridge in the process. Were Josh to then have sex with "Amy" several hours later, it is possible that some of the displaced semen from Mike would still be present under his foreskin and thus may be unwittingly transmitted to Amy who, in turn, could then be impregnated by Mike's sperm.

It's not exactly an immaculate conception. But just imagine the look on Maury Povich's face.

The Vagina Dialogues
Johanna Gohmann

This past November, two women wearing giant plush vulva costumes were shouting on a street corner in New York City. But they weren't trying to reel in tourists; these vulvas had a purpose. They were standing in front of the Manhattan Center for Vaginal Surgery, performing a short play entitled *Dr. Interest-Free Financing and the Two Vulvas,* part of a creative, eye-catching protest against vaginal cosmetic surgery. There was even a brief cameo from a giant pair of scissors.

Fifteen years ago, "The Designer Vagina" would simply have been a good name for a band. Now, vaginal cosmetic surgery is the fastest-growing cosmetic procedure in the U.K. While there are still only about a thousand surgeries done each year in the U.S., there was a 30 percent increase in 2005 alone. The numbers could actually be even higher, but data is still scarce. More and more women are opting to have their labia snipped off and "sculpted" through labiaplasty, or their vaginas stitched smaller and tighter with vaginal rejuvenation. These women are of all ages, many in their early twenties. Even scarier, some surgeons have conducted consultations with patients as young as fifteen.

What the hell is going on here? Who are these women, and what is pushing them to the extreme of slicing up their lady flower? As with anything involving our sexuality, the answer is complex, and a number of factors are at play. But the most common reason women give for wanting labiaplasty is, of course, cosmetic. Simply put, they want a "prettier" vagina. (And yes, I know the vagina is actually only the interior tract, but I'm using the word in the colloquial sense.) We live in the age of the Britney vadge flash, thongs, Brazilian waxes, and "sexting." With that much crotch on display, it's not surprising that the concept of an "ideal vagina" has emerged. But what exactly is it? When asked to describe such a thing, many of us would probably be at a loss. One that shoots out gold coins? Or can whistle Prince on cue?

Some women are quite clear on what makes for a perfect vagina—they believe it can be found in porn and bring centerfolds to their surgeons for reference. As the website for the Laser Vaginal Rejuvenation Institute of Manhattan proclaims: "Many people have asked us for an example of an aesthetically pleasing vagina. We went to our patients for the answer, and they said the playmates of *Playboy*." Other docs concur that porn is the gold standard. Gary Alter is a Beverly Hills–based surgeon who has perfected his own "After Labia Minora Contouring Technique." He says, "The widespread viewing of pornographic photos and videos has lead to a marked rise in female genital cosmetic surgery. Women are more aware of differences in genital appearance, so they wish to achieve their perceived aesthetic ideal."

Viewing vaginas in porn as "the ideal," however, poses a

number of problems. For starters, the majority of mainstream porn magazines and videos show only one very specific type of crotch—the perfect pink clam. Women with large or asymmetrical inner labia don't get a lot of room or airtime. (Interestingly enough, this doesn't always have to do with aesthetics. Sometimes it's a question of censorship laws—inner labia are deemed more "provocative," and by not showing them, a mag can get a "softer" rating. *Playboy* is known for tucking in or airbrushing away labia.) So actually, Dr. Alter, women are not so aware of differences in genital appearance. While lesbians are probably a bit more informed, many women aren't familiar with the look of regular, everyday vaginas, which come in an endless range of shapes and sizes. If you're straight, it's very likely your vadge knowledge is limited to a squat with a hand mirror, or Jenna Jameson. Maybe you also had a diagrammed health-book drawing to stare at or a gym teacher who drew a crooked vulva on the blackboard. But Coach Sartini certainly never barked at me, "And by the way, Gohmann, there are all kinds of labes out there! Long ones, hidden ones, asymmetrical ones, all kinds! Got that?"

The vagina has long been shrouded in mystery and shame for many women. Thankfully, Eve Ensler's *The Vagina Monologues* did a lot to break our culture's vadge code of silence. As she so eloquently remarks in the play's opening: "There's so much darkness and secrecy surrounding them—like the Bermuda Triangle. Nobody ever reports back from there." Sadly it appears we're still doing a pretty crappy job of reporting back if some women are using *Barely Legal* as a gauge for what is "ideal." But if some women believe that's what men find attractive, they're willing to do whatever it takes to be "hot."

However, through the course of my research, I encountered, time and again, men who say they really "do not care" what a woman's vadge looks like. The general sentiment seemed to be that any vagina is a good vagina. Obviously, some men must care, or there would be more diversity in porn. But has their preference been programmed by porn, or vice versa? Personally, I think any man who calls a vagina "ugly" needs to be handed a photo of his testicles and sent packing, but unfortunately, not everyone feels this way.

Yet not all women are getting labiaplasty for men. Or at least, so they claim. I spoke with Melissa, a bright and bubbly twenty-four-year-old from California, who carefully researched her labiaplasty and breast implants, which she had done on the same day. Melissa was not only adamant that she wasn't doing it "for a man," but she also seemed rather insulted by the idea: "I don't care if men like my nail polish color, and I certainly don't care if men like my vision of an ideal vagina." Melissa insists her desire for surgery mainly had to do with physical discomfort. Though she's completely healthy with perfectly normal anatomy, Melissa's labia were causing her pain—another major reason women list for getting labiaplasty. Some women with bigger labia say they become sore from too much time on the exercise bike, they feel tender after sex, or that certain underwear "doesn't fit right." While these problems are pretty universal for women, long labes or not, some feel it's worthy of surgical intervention. In Melissa's case, her labia were interfering with her passion for horseback riding. But she also admits to being a "perfectionist," and after she made up her mind to get the surgery, she wanted to "look stellar down there." She scanned porn sites to find the right "look," then trolled before-and-after albums at cosmetic-surgery sites like MakeMeHeal.com. She found only a few "after" shots that suited her, and expressed surprise that "most people wanted their doctor to leave more labia than I even had to begin with!" Melissa ultimately ended up getting what is known as "the Barbie Doll look," or "the youth/preteen look": she had all of her inner labia removed.

Plastic surgeon John Di Saia asserts that these surgeries are helpful to women and believes the practice has merely been sensationalized in the media. He used to do about three labiaplasties a month, but in the current economy, he performs less than a dozen a year. (Wow. This really is like the Great Depression. Who will pen our *Labes of Wrath?*) In an email interview, I asked him about the validity of labia interfering with women's exercise, and he responded, "Some patients cannot wear tight clothing because of the discomfort. That is not normal." But he then went on to say, "In borderline cases, you may have a point, as each patient justifies her decision differently. Some women just don't like the way their Labiae [*sic*] look. They want them looking tighter, smaller, and frequently more oval-shaped."

It would seem that when "physical problems" are cited as reasoning for surgery, they are often closely intertwined with the cosmetic. And when those problems have to do with sexual dysfunction, the line between the physical and the cosmetic becomes even more blurred. In 2004, Dr. Laura Berman, director of the Berman Center (a treatment clinic for female sexual dysfunction) completed a study on the relationship between women's genital self-mage and their sexual function. She surveyed 2,206 women and, not surprisingly, found that the way you feel about your vadge plays a huge part in how much you enjoy sex. But rather than helping women deal with dysfunction by teaching them about their bodies and working toward overcoming esteem issues, our cultural response is to offer surgery as the solution. Doctors will simply trim away your "ugly" bits.

"It's promoted with claims of increased sexual pleasure,

increased self-confidence, and a 'better' aesthetic appearance. These are seductive and sound good—who wouldn't want better self-esteem or a better sex life?" says Virginia Braun, a psychologist and senior lecturer in psychology at The University of Auckland, New Zealand. She has been studying female genital cosmetic surgery since 2002. She points out that the claims these surgeons make "are not evidence-based, although they are presented as if they were facts—what will happen to you if you have the surgery." So despite there being no real evidence (a formal medical study has never been done), many surgeons are loudly proclaiming the surgeries as a cure for your bedroom woes. The tricky thing is that in some cases, it's true. But this is where the snake starts to swallow its tail. Dr. Di Saia himself probably explains it best: "Sexual response is frequently increased, but I think this has to do with comfort. Women tend to have a much more cerebral experience with sex than men do. Self-consciousness or worry of pain can stop things in their tracks, and nobody wants that." I think we can all agree that women have a more cerebral response to sex. But that seems to be the crux of the problem. Women are slicing off parts of their sex organs in the hopes of having better sex. Before we raise the scalpels, it seems going to the source—the cerebrum—would be a much better option.

Unfortunately, that's not nearly as easy as a one-hour outpatient procedure performed under local anesthesia. A root canal takes longer! A simple Google search offers a slew of websites promising the "solution" to your vagina problems, whether your sex life sucks, you're training for the Tour de France, or you're convinced your vagina is straight out of "Cloverfield." Many of the sites look like they're advertising a relaxing spa treatment, not a procedure that ends in dissolvable stitches. They call the surgery "empowering!" And something you can "do for yourself!"

LabiaplastySurgeon.com explains that the surgery is a good choice for "women who are experiencing sexual dysfunction, embarrassment, or pain because their labia minora are oversized or asymmetrical." It states surgery is also for "women who dislike their large labia or shape of their labia, which may cause inelegance or awkwardness with a sexual partner." That's right, ladies! Dr. Bernard Stern wants to save you and your big, floppy labia from an inelegant moment in the bedroom. Extra helpful are the sites's many before and after photos. On the left is a perfectly normal vulva; on the right is the same vulva, now trimmed of all that inelegant, nerve-filled tissue that can greatly contribute to a woman's sexual pleasure. If you still aren't sold, check out the loads of online "success" stories from past patients who make the surgery sound as easy as a belly piercing. And almost every doctor offers a "free consultation!"

I tracked down a local clinic that offered labiaplasty and met with Michelle, a lovely registered nurse in her midtwenties. I gave her my made-up spiel about why I wanted labiaplasty, emphasizing that I had no physical problems whatsoever but just didn't like the way I looked. "Many women have it strictly for cosmetic reasons," she assured me. "It's about making you feel better about yourself!" She then gave me a sunny presentation about how simple it was, how attentive they would be, and how I needn't feel embarrassed. I listened to her very convincing pitch, after which I asked about possible side effects, like nerve damage or loss of sensitivity. "Oh," she said, looking sincerely befuddled. "I've never heard of anything like that happening here. Really, it's such a simple procedure. But you could ask the doctor at your next appointment." With that cleared up, she slipped into hard-sell mode and pulled up her online calendar to book my follow-up. By the time I left the office, I almost felt excited for my pretend surgery.

It's all so easy! Like getting my teeth whitened. Sure, it was going to cost me $5,934, but really, I should have done it years ago! I could only imagine what it must be like for women who truly are ashamed of their vagina and who encounter the bright-eyed, Noxzema-clean Michelle, who promises such a quick and simple solution to their woes.

While it's not hard to find a doctor happy to perform labiaplasty, it's a bit tougher to find info on how safe the surgery is—as exemplified by my free consultation. And this is because no one really knows. Again, no long-term studies have ever been done. Websites and doctors downplay possible side effects and instead list "mild discomfort and swelling" as the main things to worry about. In 2007, The American College of Obstetricians and Gynecologists issued a statement that the surgery is "not medically indicated," and that it is "deceptive to give the impression that vaginal rejuvenation, designer vaginoplasty, revirginization, G-spot amplification or any other such procedures are accepted and routine surgical practices." They offer a frightening list of potential complications, including "infection, altered sensitivity, dyspareunia, adhesions, and scarring." The surgeries were also blacklisted by The Royal Australian and New Zealand College of Obstetricians and Gynecologists after doctors saw an increase in women needing reconstructive surgery due to badly botched jobs. They issued a statement saying the procedures are "not very anatomically based and have the potential to cause serious harm."

So despite the lack of a formal study, there is little doubt that these surgeries can be incredibly risky and can come with grave complications. But it's tough to find anyone who will open up about a procedure gone wrong—no one wants to be the cover girl for bungled vagina surgery. Even our reigning queen of vaginas, Jenna Jameson, was close-mouthed about her experience; when the famed porn star reportedly underwent a vaginoplasty in 2007, she was supposedly so upset with the results that she went into hiding. And when a woman with an "ideal" vagina is getting vaginoplasty, we've got a problem.

There are a handful of organizations and individuals who are trying to tip the information scale in the other direction, letting women know there are roads to empowerment that don't involve incisions. Most notable is The New View Campaign (www.fsd-alert.org), a group dedicated to "challenging the medicalization of sex" and the organizers of the aforementioned vulva play. Its website provides an extensive overview of vaginoplasty, as well as links to books and videos on women's sexual health and dysfunction. The group has a long list of endorsements from various doctors and social scientists; it even gets the thumbs-up from former prostitute turned sex guru and performance artist Annie Sprinkle. Its latest efforts include The International Vulva Knitting Circle, a playful way to bring women together to talk about their bodies and knit vulvas. So far there are circles in Brooklyn, Melbourne, Toronto, and Auckland, with hopes to exhibit a global collection of the handiwork in New York next year.

Offering a male perspective on the subject is British artist Jamie McCartney, who's educating people on vadge variety with a piece called *Design a Vagina*. He is making two hundred casts of volunteers' lady parts and will be hanging them together in large panels. (I had the opportunity to participate as a volunteer and see McCartney's work—let's just say it made a lasting impression.) McCartney hopes his sculpture will eventually find a home in a public space, saying, "for many women, their vagina is a source of shame rather than pride, and this piece seeks to redress the balance, showing that everyone is different, and everyone is normal."

For the younger ladies, there is Scarleteen.com, a fabulous site that offers "sex ed for the real world." In its "Give 'Em Some Lip: Labia That Clearly Ain't Minor" section, the site answers young women's questions about what a "normal" vagina looks like and provides helpful pictures and diagrams, including a link to the eye-opening drawings of Betty Dodson, a regular contributor to *BUST*.

So there are a few voices yelling into the void, people working to follow Ensler's edict to "spread the word." And while some women might cringe at the idea of vagina sculptures and labia costumes and vulva cozies, they would no doubt prefer them to the proliferation of perfectly healthy women putting their most intimate body part under the knife for a potentially dangerous, unnecessary procedure. As it stands now, any means to bridge the gap between the mass of swirling misinformation and the truth should be welcomed, since what we have are the conditions for a perfect storm. With a lack of education and information, a built-in cultural shame surrounding vaginas, a preponderance of false images in the media, and a line of medical professionals taking our signed checks and nodding reassuringly, in five years' time, will getting a streamlined vagina be as common as a tummy tuck?

As The New View Campaign points out: just as the fight to rid Africa of female genital mutilation is gaining real momentum, the West appears to be picking up the very knives they are putting down. And yes, there are numerous differences between FGM and labiaplasty. But there is also the eerie similarity that both are born of cultural standards imposed upon the women of the society. While our surgeries may be done entirely by choice, one wonders at what point the disconnect occurs between denouncing the use of a scalpel by others and then picking it up ourselves.

Sex Laws That Can Really Screw You
Ellen Friedrichs

The older I get, the luckier I feel not to have been busted for breaking a sex law. It's not that I have been doing anything particularly scandalous. Public sex sure isn't my thing, and I'm not in the habit of spamming my friends and colleagues with XXX emails. But in a world where a teen can get arrested for texting a boyfriend her own nudie shots, I don't want to take anything for granted.

Really though, my clean record probably has as much to do with where I've lived, as with what I've done. Growing up in Canada meant that I didn't worry about the legal ramifications of losing my virginity to my high school boyfriend. Had I spent those angst-ridden years in Texas, or even Maine, I could have been charged with the crime of underage sex.

Similarly, accompanying a terrified sixteen-year-old to a New York City clinic for an abortion a few years back could have been illegal if I had done the same thing in many of the thirty-four states with parental consent and notification laws for this procedure. So I've been fortunate. But plenty of other people haven't. We often don't realize that sex regulations extend beyond archaic blue laws banning things like having sex in a toll booth, or forbidding sororities on the basis that women living together constitute a brothel. Such prohibitions may remain on the books, but people seldom, if ever, face charges for breaking them. The sex laws that do get enforced every day tend to be a lot less laughable.

Occasionally, the focus on a particular case can lead to a law's repeal. For example, in 2004, a Texas mom was arrested for violating that state's ban on selling sex toys after she was busted hawking vibrators to her friends. The coverage of the incident drew attention to the statute and eventually led to its 2008 nullification. And famously, following a 2002 arrest for having anal sex with his boyfriend, John Lawrence argued his case before the U. S. Supreme Court, and succeeded in getting the federal sodomy laws overturned.

Nevertheless, for many people, simply paying their fine or doing their time is preferable to embarrassing publicity that can accompany fighting charges. Still, plenty of cases do make the papers, whether those involved want them to or not.

Here are fifteen recent examples highlighting the fact that even in the land of the free, the freedom to express your sexuality can still be pretty limited.

1) Over the past year, New York City has seen thirty-four gay men arrested for prostitution in what many people are calling an antigay sting operation. One case, reported by the *New York Times,* involved Robert Pinter, a fifty-three-year-old massage therapist, who was approached by an undercover police officer in the adult section of a video store. As Pinter told the *Times,* "[the man who

propositioned me] was very charming and cute, and we agreed to leave the store and engage in consensual sex." Pinter explained that man then offered him fifty dollars for doing so—an offer which he says he did not respond to. Once outside, Pinter was handcuffed and arrested on charges of "loitering for the purpose of prostitution." The relationship between gay men and the police has often been far from harmonious (hell, arrests of gay men in the sixties are what prompted the Stonewall riots in 1969), and this situation has renewed fears that old habits die hard.

2) Despite the fact that Georgia has some real problems with youth sexual health—among other things it boasts the eighth highest teen pregnancy rate in the country—this state has put a lot more effort into targeting teens than it has into helping them stay safe. One particularly outlandish case involves a young man named Genarlow Wilson. Genarlow was recently freed after serving almost three years in a Georgia prison. He had been sent there at seventeen for getting a blow job from a consenting fifteen-year-old girl. Though Genarlow was only two years older than the girl, in Georgia, he was above the age of consent and she was below it. As a result, the high school senior was charged with aggravated child molestation. At the time, Georgia had a mandatory minimum sentence of ten years for this crime, so that's what he got. A year into his sentence, the law was changed to make the maximum penalty a still pretty serious twelve months in jail. Even so, it took another two years for a judge to order Genarlow's release.

3) Florida is famous for its liberal views on how little clothing can be considered publicly acceptable. It's not so liberal, however, when it comes to the kind of sex it considers acceptable for people to have privately. In February, a lawsuit was filed against a strip mall–based private swingers club. The charges came after

a year-long undercover operation, and despite the sheriff's acknowledgment that "detectives never found any evidence of drug use or sales and never saw any instances of anyone paying for sex." Swinging is legal, so in the end, the best the cops could do was charge the club with violation of local zoning codes.

4) Starting off 2009 with a bang, six Pennsylvania teens—three girls and three boys—were busted for child pornography. The charges came after a teacher confiscated a student's cell phone and discovered that the girls had sent naked pictures of themselves to the boys. Initially, the boys were charged with possession of child pornography, and the girls with manufacturing, disseminating and possessing child pornography. These charges could have come with jail time and the requirement to register as sex offenders. The AP reports, given such daunting prospects, "all but one of the students accepted a lesser misdemeanor charge, partly to avoid a trial and further embarrassment." Public panic over sexting is growing and as a result the Pennsylvania case is far from an isolated incident. In fact, USA Today reports that, "Police have investigated more than two dozen teens in at least six states this year for sending nude images of themselves in cell phone text messages."

5) No one has ever claimed that Georgia is a haven for the LGBT community. But a recent decision by a custody judge to bar a gay dad from "exposing" his kids to his "homosexual partners and friends," is a reminder that in this state, the notion that everyone is equal under the law only applies if the "everyone" in question isn't gay. In this case, the man's soon to be ex-wife argued that the fact that her kids have a gay dad has landed them in therapy. So she asked that the restriction be imposed to protect them from discomfort. But as the father said, "In general, that [restriction] will never allow me to have my children present

in front of any friends, whether they're gay or straight—no one hands you a card saying are you gay, straight, heterosexual, bi, whatever."

6) After his boxers were spotted by cops as he peddled his bike around town, a twenty-four-year-old Bainbridge, Georgia, man became the first person arrested there under a new city ordinance that prohibits wearing pants low enough to expose a person's underwear. Arrests like this have become common all over the country as more and more cities adopt so-called *baggy pants bans*. Most of these laws focus on visible underwear. But some, like the one passed in Lafourche Parish, Louisiana, in 2007, take the clothing restrictions even further. That ordinance not only outlaws "any indecent exposure of any person or undergarments," but also bars a person from, "dressing in a manner not becoming to his or her sex."

7) Last February, Wisconsin mom Amy Smalley was charged with the felony of "exposing a child to harmful descriptions." The issue came to light after her eleven-year-old son told a counselor about conversations his mom had with him and his brother. These included talking about her sex life, explaining how to perform oral sex and showing the boys a sex toy. The charges, which could have landed Smalley three years in prison, were pled down to a misdemeanor. Smalley was placed on probation and had to undergo court-ordered counseling. As the Court TV website put it, "Smalley called it education. Prosecutors called it a crime." I call it terrifying. As a mom myself, I can easily see having similar conversations. (Okay, not for a while as my daughter is only two. But still...) Sure, Smalley probably made a bad judgment call. But really, is this any worse than parents who let their kids watch "Family Guy" and "South Park," despite the endless stream of rape jokes and blow job humor?

8) In 2010, a law designed to protect child prostitutes will take effect in New York State. Until that time, kids as young as twelve can continue to be charged with the crime of prostitution. This is true even if they were forced into the business by pimps. Interestingly, since 2000, foreign-born teens have been protected from prosecution by anti-trafficking laws that view them as victims. For the next year, however, teens with American citizenship may still find themselves in juvie for being the victim of something most people would consider pretty horrific abuse. Hopefully, this is a sign that we are making progress not only on the issue of sex work, but on the treatment of juvenile offenders in general.

9) In December 2008, a Florida woman reacted to the penis being forced into her mouth by biting. Twenty-seven-year-old Charris Bowers told police that despite the fact that she didn't want to have oral sex, her husband, Delou, pushed himself into her mouth, and that she clamped down to get him to stop. He responded by punching her in the head until she let go. In the end no charges were filed against Delou, even though it is illegal for anyone, including a spouse, to make another person perform a sex act. Charris, on the other hand, was arrested and charged with battery. Apparently, blaming the victims of sexual assault is not a thing of the past.

10) That sexual double standards for men and women are alive and well shouldn't come as a shock to anyone. But a Wisconsin town recently showed just how damaging such notions can be. On consecutive January days in Sheboygan, Wisconsin, seventeen-year-old Norma Guthrie and seventeen-year-old Alan Jepsen were charged with sexual assault for having consensual sex with their fourteen-year-old partners. However, that's where the similarities between the cases end. Guthrie was charged with a misdemeanor, which carries a maximum nine months in prison.

Jepsen, on the other hand, was charged with a felony, which carries a maximum twenty-five years in prison. The *Sheboygan Press* reports, "Assistant District Attorney Jim Haasch, who filed both complaints, said the misdemeanor charge was filed in part because Guthrie has no prior criminal record. But online court records show Guthrie has a pending charge of misdemeanor battery, filed in October. Haasch would not say whether Jepsen has a prior juvenile record—which is typically sealed—but the boy has no adult charges listed in online court records. Haasch also said the cases are different because Guthrie's boyfriend is 'almost fifteen,' with a birthday in February. Jepsen's girlfriend turns fifteen in April."

11) In December, something called a *paramour clause* was used to force a lesbian in Tennessee to move out of her house and away from her family. The clause prohibits cohabitation of unmarried partners if minor children are in the home. In this particular situation, the lesbian couple had lived together for over ten years. Much of that was with the biological mom's kids, who were the product of a previous relationship with a man. There was no indication that this living situation was harming the thirteen- and fifteen-year-old teens. Nor had the father requested that his ex's partner move out. Still, a custody judge imposed the rule, leaving few options for the women in a state where same sex couples cannot legally marry. And people wonder why Proposition 8 matters?

12) As a sex ed teacher, I believe in answering teens' questions honestly and in using language that they will relate to and understand. So had I overheard a conversation between a New York State high school teacher and some of her students, I probably would have applauded her candor. But I didn't get wind of this conversation. Josephine Isernia's school board did. According to

the board, when asked for advice on oral sex by one of the girls, Isernia used words that were, "vulgar, obscene and disgusting." The words in question? *Head job, hand job* and *fellatio*. Isernia was a teacher with over twenty years of experience who had never been in trouble before. Yet despite her clean record and the fact that the students sought her out for information, when 2009 rolled around, she was out of a job and educators everywhere were given a sad wake-up call.

13) Remember a few years back when PDA policies were making the news every other day? Lately stories about sexting and moms who pose as teens on MySpace have been stealing the headlines. But rules regarding public displays of affection never really went away and this February, twenty-two-year-old Jessica Garcia was arrested at her local mall for kissing her girlfriend. According to Garcia, mall security told the couple, "This is a family mall, y'all can't do this. Y'all kissed, and if y'all do it again I'm going to write you a citation or I'm going to kick y'all out." The mall countered that after being asked to leave following the kiss, the couple returned and became belligerent. This, a mall spokesperson claimed, and not the kiss, is what led to the arrest. Regardless, Garcia is considering suing for discrimination.

14) Imagine this: You're sixteen and having sex with your boyfriend. You want to be safe so you ask your mom to take you to the doctor for birth control. Most people would call this a sign of maturity and responsibility. The state of Mississippi would call it an incident to be reported to the cops. That's because a bill that passed in January makes it a crime for parents *not* to report to the police that their kids are having sex. The Mississippi Child Protection Act of 2009, requires mandatory reporting of sex crimes against children and imposes new abortion restrictions on minors. Though there is much to quibble with in the bill, one

section is particularly alarming. This is the clause that prohibits, "the intentional toleration of a parent or caretaker of the child's sexual involvement *with any other person.*" Supporters of the law claim that they are trying to protect young people from abuse. But nowhere does the bill distinguish between sexual abuse and consensual sexual encounters between teens. Mississippi already boasts the highest teen pregnancy rate in the country. Maybe they are striving for the number one spot in preventing parent/child communication, as well....

15) This past November, a convicted sex offender in Oklahoma had little reason to celebrate having his criminal record expunged. That's because the requirement that he register as a sex offender for life remained. This is particularly problematic seeing as the individual in question is a kid. Due to age of consent laws, he was convicted at sixteen of having consensual sex with a thirteen-year-old girl. His mother explains that sex offender status meant the boy was, "removed from high school [and] prohibited from being in the presence of children other than his younger brother. He can't go near schools, day care centers or parks. His brother, age eleven, can't bring friends into their home. If his brother had been a girl, Ricky [the offender] would have been removed from his home." The United States has some of the toughest sex offender laws in the world and Ricky is far from the only teen forced to live under such conditions. As Human Rights Watch reports, "Some children are on registries because they committed serious sex offenses, such as forcibly raping a much younger child. Other children are labeled sex offenders for such noncoercive or nonviolent and age-appropriate activities as "playing doctor," youthful pranks such as exposing one's buttocks, and noncoercive teen sex."

There has been talk recently about America's liberalizing mo-

mercial? The one with the jingle "Hold the pickles, hold the lettuce; special orders don't upset us..." It was kind of like that. As a guy in this business, you're surrounded by thousands of ads in which the escorts reduce themselves to a handful of stock ad copy, passing their bodies off as fast cars worthy of worship and frequent waxing. I was never interested in being that kind of car. I always saw myself as a Toyota Camry: attractive but not showy; reliable and practical. This is an indication of how deeply entrenched I am in the capitalist machinery. I'm a Camry. I say this voluntarily, I am a Camry.

It's certainly better in the age of Internet advertising. In the old days, when guys ran print ads, each word was extra money. Those print ads were haiku. Three lines of text. Something along the lines of:

> *Swimmer's build, a body guys love to service,*
> *Hung top, young and fun, clean,*
> *No attitude.*

In any given ad, a potential client could be triggered by a single word: "athletic" might mean that the escort would be willing to reenact a client's childhood trauma of nearly drowning and being resuscitated by a lifeguard's hour-long certification training in CPR. The word "service" might mean that the escort was straight and possibly married at some point, with small children in some other state. A man's children are sexy only when they reside elsewhere. The print ad format created a social dynamic wherein the escort became a projection screen for every fear and fantasy the client could possibly have. It was all so open-ended, the way someone's identity was compressed into fifteen words. *He sounds like an ex-con. Maybe he's a nice kid putting himself through college*. The whole enterprise was a giant guessing game.

The Internet has mitigated this situation somewhat. On the Web, escorts have more room to spread out. Surprisingly few take advantage of this liberty. It's the sad dilemma of democracy: we as a people have all this leeway and we do nothing with it. Even on a website where one is afforded five hundred words of text, you see the same clipped language, the same numbers and stats and meaningless phrases like "no attitude." Why would someone say they had no attitude? It's like saying you don't have an ego. You do. The question is not whether you have an attitude or an ego. The question is whether you're a conceited prick. Attitude and ego are conditions, not unlike the weather. Can you imagine the tourist bureau of a vacation spot bragging that the island has "no weather?"

I never had one of those ads, which seem to be written by people with no sentences at their disposal whatsoever. English as a third or fourth language. All of that said, I am reluctant to set down the exact text of my ad because I've built it up into this mythic, messianic sacred text. Like it's not on the goddamn Internet at all; rather it's on a scroll that you unroll with the help of two clerics. At the risk of being overly simplistic, I'll say that all I did was use complete sentences. We live in an age of fission. All around us, the language is being split into tiny, marketable pieces. Three-second chunks of information—visual media is edited in such a way that we're all careening toward epilepsy. Meanwhile, the sentence is an old friend. The sentence is a familiar revolution. I trust the sentence.

Okay, I'll give you a few of the sentences, but I'm changing the text, because I'm still out there working. I am not writing about some quaint indiscretion of youth. This is how I make my living. Here's a short piece of my ad:

I have a rolling suitcase of toys and erotic clothes I can bring to your hotel room or home; if you want, we can play with what's there, or you can just look through it. I've seen or imagined damn near everything, so if you've got a fantasy that's particularly out there, it's only going to delight me. Why not? You might as well.

The new clients who came to me after I ran that ad were hungry men. They were a varied lot, but they had a few things in common. Many had been through unsatisfying experiences with other escorts who didn't accommodate their peculiar fantasies and in some cases shamed them for asking in the first place. Another thing these clients had in common was a sense of devotion. They'd carried these secrets for many years, enacting their fetish lives in private. They'd kept bags of lingerie hidden in a shoebox in the basement. They'd hidden porn videos under floorboards. They'd gotten ashamed and thrown everything away, only to regather a new set of taboo items. To me, they were heroic, like the people in *Fahrenheit 451* who memorize books to preserve literature. Erotic freedom by any means necessary.

I'm thinking of one client in particular—Ray. Most clients use their real names, I've found. You can tell when a client is using a made-up name because it's more generic than their actual name. For instance, when a client named Ethan picks a fake name, he picks Joe. When an escort named Joe picks a hooker name, he selects Ethan. That says it all.

Ray was staying at the St. Francis in this really big suite. Visiting from Texas, although I wouldn't find that out until several sessions later. You know that stereotype about how clients want to tell you all their problems, so much so that you don't spend very much time having sex? The sex worker as talk therapist? It's complete bullshit. It makes non–sex workers feel less threatened by the concept of sex for pay. Like when the government invades a country and launches a media disinformation campaign so people think the troops are just there keeping the peace, when really they're carrying out midnight raids and razing apartment buildings and shooting civilians point-blank. I grew up in a military family. I know that's what really happens because the men in my family are all emotionally unavailable. That's what happens when you murder small children in the name of God and country. Veterans are a trip as clients. I don't even want to go into that right now. I want to stay with Ray.

Ray and I communicated solely by email before meeting. He hired me for an overnight and often I like to confirm those sorts of appointments by phone, just to make sure the guy's for real. However, I got such an honest, gentle vibe from Ray's email that a phone call wasn't necessary. In addition, I really love the surprise of seeing who's behind the hotel room door. I know sex workers who require the clients to send them pictures and ask for stats and all of that. They don't like suspense. They want to know what they're getting into. For me it's a deeper practice to arrive with very little to go on. The clients who don't give you any hints at all—no phone voice, no age, nothing. Those are the guys I end up learning the most from. Especially if they're not traditionally handsome. Maybe they've got some extra weight, maybe their skin has red patches, maybe they have a micropenis. If there's some characteristic that renders them defective in the eyes of the culture, it makes me more excited to play with them. Like when a firefighter gets a call for a five-alarm blaze. It's exciting. It's a challenge. I feel like I'm being of service in a larger context, that I'm transmitting ancient sex wisdom to people who need it badly and are cut off from it. That's a grand assessment, certainly. No grander, I would argue, than saying you're a man of God. No grander than stepping forward to teach our nation's children. No grander than signing up to bear arms so that you can preserve civility itself. I take my job seriously.

When I arrived, Ray greeted me warmly, extending his hand to shake. Very few clients shake your hand. Some grab you and kiss you right away, but nobody shakes your hand. Every now and then a client will want to meet you in the lobby. Usually they want to make sure it's a match, or they feel safer meeting you in a public place. It makes it easier for them to back out at the last minute. Ray had none of these hang-ups. I'm just giving you a frame of reference. Ray was a hand shaker in world full of quick-to-kiss men.

I sat down on a loveseat in the living room area of his suite. He appeared to be around fifty years old, just a few years shy of the client median age.

"Can I offer you anything?" he asked.

"No, I'm fine," I said. This is my automatic Southern response. Then he's supposed to tell me what he actually has to offer. Then I refuse again. Then he tells me what he's having and would I care to join him. As a Southerner, that's when it's okay to accept a drink from a stranger.

"I've got wine and beer, soda and bottled water."

"I think I'm okay."

"I've got a bottle of white wine already open."

"That sounds lovely."

He poured me a glass of chardonnay. I'm sure it was expensive. The nuance of fine spirits is entirely lost on me. As an alcohol drinker, I cut my teeth on Sun Country wine cooler from two-liter bottles. We'd be lying on hillsides overlooking dirt roads out in the county, passing the bottle around. Just about everything tastes expensive to me.

Ray had these massive blue irises that were too big for his body. Babies have those sorts of eyes and then their faces catch up. He had a sweet Texas lilt—in the South, many men and women have the same gentle vocal mannerisms. The desire to please crosses gender lines. Ray was no exception. As we talked during that first visit, whenever I said something remotely agreeable, he'd say "Aren't you kind to say that" or "Bless your heart." I felt like I was ten years old, serving triangular finger sandwiches at my mother's luncheon. It's delicate when you first meet someone for sex. You want to ease into familiarity with them, but you don't want to be so chatty that you kill the mysterious sexual energy that exists between you.

After about half an hour of conversation, Ray abruptly pulled out a bag of nylon hose and Lycra shorts and dress socks. Via email, he'd said he wanted a witness, that he wanted to show me what he'd been doing over the years. It's tricky, when someone offers you the raw components of their desire. You ought to be supportive, but you don't want to be a cheerleading mom about it either. They're going to the underworld, for Christ's sake. Your job is not to gush over their watercolor and tape it to the refrigerator door. Your job is to go to the underworld with them.

Ray showed me the bag. "This is my passion, right here."

I could see both men's and women's stockings, tight athletic clothing and the like. He had a penchant for the enclosure offered by elastic fabric. It didn't seem like he wanted to kiss yet or interact physically, so I asked him to do a fashion show for me. I put it in more masculine terms. I asked him to show off for me. I told him I wanted to see him slowly take every single piece of clothing off, fold them neatly on a chair, then put on every single piece of clothing in that bag. I was just hazarding a guess, but as it turns out, this was precisely his fetish—the pileup of stretchable layers, one upon another. As he stripped down, I could see his hairy back and his short stocky legs. He had an enormous cock, the kind that doesn't grow too much in an erect state. I had a boyfriend with a cock like that once and he ruined me for getting fucked by anyone else for several years. It took willpower for me not to jump Ray right then, grease him up and slide his cock into my ass. Ray needed me to suspend my interest in his penis and bring all my focus to his wardrobe. A cardinal rule of gay male escorting is Don't Give Them Bottom Energy Unless They Specifically Ask For It. So I sat back and admired him in all his overgrown splendor.

He narrated his assemblage of clothing, which amused me and turned me on. I love a dirty talker more than anything. It's a skill I've never really developed. I've tried and I just feel silly. So when someone goes for it, assigning in-the-moment language to their behavior, I'm all for it. It seems like a huge blind spot in a sex healer's skill set, the gift of dirty gab, but I make up for it with other forms of fearlessness.

"These black stockings," Ray said, "I bought on sale at Bloomingdale's. The woman who helped me asked if I wanted to try them on. Didn't even assume they were for my wife. This was in New York. You know how they are in New York."

I nodded. I knew exactly how they are in New York.

"In the dressing room, they pushed my cock down so much that I leaked precum right away. I was supposed to try them on over my underwear but I didn't. So I had to buy them. They're so thick that I've never had a run."

He turned his ass toward me, which the hose pushed up and out as if it was a shelf you could put drinks on. This was confusing the bottom part of me that was still fixated on his big floppy dick. Because now, more than anything, I wanted to fuck Ray.

"Hey Ray—I'd love to cut a hole in your stockings and fuck you right through them."

"No," he said, "I love these stockings too much. Maybe we can go shopping and find some that I wouldn't mind cutting. These are sacred to me."

Ray pulled on a pair of lacy pink panties over his panty hose, then immediately followed that with a pair of white Lycra biker shorts. You could see the lace bunching under the shorts. His bulge looked artificial, like a lead singer from a hair metal band. Like a superhero. Ray was my little superhero.

He pulled on a bra and came over to me so I could help him fasten the back.

"I can do all of this myself but I thought you might like to help."

"Do you want to be my little girlfriend?" I asked.

"No," he said, "we're a couple of guys and I'm trying things on for you."

Leave it to this Texan to have a way more complicated gender identity than a professional San Franciscan could articulate.

"Good for you, Ray," I said. "You're fuckin' beautiful."

Ray pulled a spandex T-shirt, the classic circuit-party gay-boy kind, over his torso.

"I want you to lick me through the elastic," he said. "Lick me so hard I feel your spit sinking through the fabric."

"Sure thing," I said, standing up with my tongue at the ready.

"But not right now," Ray said. "I just got started."

Ray continued putting on every article of clothing in the bag. He pulled on a pair of gold gloves that reached up past his biceps. He tucked the ends under his T-shirt and then put on a black spandex hood with two eyeholes and an opening for his mouth. That did it. He was completely covered. He stood there, panting out the mouth hole in his mask. He turned and faced me, holding his hands up into the air like a victorious Mexican wrestler. Humble. Brave.

I lifted my wineglass in a toast, then took a gulp. Ray kept his arms up over his head. I wasn't sure if he was offering himself up to God or the Devil, but I think either way, it was a hell of a gesture. I wasn't sure what he wanted me to do. I wanted to clap or tie him up or something to make myself useful. I decided I would take my cock out and show him how hard I was looking at him in this purest of states. I unzipped and pulled my cock through my pants. I gripped my erection and grunted a little bit, not wanting to puncture this moment with useless words. Ray started making gurgling noises, like he was just about to wake up from a nightmare, the sort of sounds you can hear yourself making to jolt yourself out of sleep. I looked at his cock and saw his cum soaking through three layers of fabric. There must have been a lot of it. It created a wet spot that grew until finally he put his hands down by his side.

"Bless your heart," Ray said. "You can go home now." He gestured to the bedside table, where there was a stack of hundred dollar bills. He was paying me for an overnight, since that's what we'd booked. I'd been there a little over two hours.

He stood, motionless. I pushed my cock back into my pants, wishing I could have at least jerked off for him. My work ethic was kicking in and I really wanted to do something for all that money.

"Thank you," he said. The way he said it made me think he wanted me to leave faster, so I went into the other room, got my overnight bag and rolled it toward the door.

"I'll call you again," Ray said. I closed the door and stepped into the hall, trying to remember whether the elevator was to the left or right. I heard the door echo through the hallway as it closed, like a buzzer signaling the shift change on a factory floor. I was thinking that the only part of Ray he'd let me touch was his hand.

BDSM and Playing with Race
Mollena Williams

I might have admired the efficiency of his movement (lean down buck knife click sick clack) drawing it into place, firm blade against my belly sluicing aside the sweat of fear and exhaustion that trickled there. I might have admired it but that I was mortally terrified. My feet, barely touching the cold, cold cement and my hands, numb and clasping in a mute upcast prayer, tied as they were to a hook above my head which pulled my shoulders painfully tight. My eyes were swollen shut from crying, throat swollen and raw from screaming, heart thudding with trip hammer speed and force and I hitched in a sobbing breath…and another and another…as the knife scraped its way up my belly, the tip intermittently alerting me to the fact that this knife meant business, yes it did, and the business was not good.

In a flash the knife was against my throat, and my head was brutally yanked to one side, and I was face-to-face with my tormentor, his otherwise jovial face twisted into a flat smile, blue eyes impossibly empty, amused, hair matted to his sweaty forehead.

"Now gal, you gonna tell me what I want to know or am I gonna cut open that lyin' throat of yours?" he drawled, and though I wanted to scream again that I had no fucking idea what he wanted me to tell him, I was past words. I just hung there limply, crying. Grabbing the nape of my neck and yanking on the hair, he twisted my head so that I looked back over my shoulder, forced me to look at the crowd gathered a few yards away.

"You see that? None of those people, not one, is gonna help you. You been kicking and screaming and no one has helped you yet, have they? Couple of 'em even helped drag your black ass back when you thought you were getting away." As I peered through eyelids heavy with tears and vision dimmed by panic, I saw that what he said was true. I could make out a crowd of people, lingering, their interest levels seeming to swing between mildly interested, to fascinated, to focused, but no one moved to help. And it was true that, hours back, when I'd been knocked down and dragged to the feet of this motherfucker, not only had no one helped me, several had helped him to restrain me, letting him beat the hell out of me, all the while insisting I had information he was gonna get, by god, or he'd call the rest of the Night Riders in and they could take turns with me.

A cold truth coiled around the base of my spine, sibilant certainty that was, strangely, a relief. *He's going to kill me,* I thought, *and I just hope he makes it fast because I can't take any more. Please god, if you are listening, make it fast. Merciful.* And I wasn't even afraid anymore. The knife had dragged its cruel intention back down my rib cage and flank, and now pressed between my legs, the tip pricking into me and I wondered how much longer it would take to bleed out if he started there. He slapped my face again, my head wedged into my shoulder didn't even move.

"Yeah. Another dead nigger. No one will give a shit. No one."

And I believed it. Even as I pleaded for mercy in my heart to a god that seems to have quietly turned away from me, I knew he was right. And hope left me.

There are as many ways to play within the BDSM community as there are people who are practitioners. From the guy who just likes to feel overpowered by his lover with hands held about his head to the hardcore pervert spending every weekend in a local dungeon in full leathers with a rolling suitcase full of gear, there are millions of people getting their freak on. And one of the pillars of BDSM play is consent, safety, and acceptance. Tolerance of other folk's proclivities is paramount to fostering a sense of community. With so much working against the person who wants to lead a lifestyle outside of the mainstream, it becomes even more critical that those who find fellowship in the alternative lifestyle have a safe space in which to explore their dark fantasies. "We must all hang together, gentlemen," quoth Benjamin Franklin, "...else, we shall most assuredly hang separately."

This truth is not so self-evident if your fantasies embrace some of the darkest and most sinister truths of human nature, and are rooted in real-life oppression.

Slavery. Genocide. Holocaust. Warfare. Racism. Hate.

These are ugly realities of life. Why would you want to plunge yourself headlong into the darkest part of the human psyche for sexual gratification? How can you know anyone well enough to know that they do not *really* believe what they are saying to you? Aren't you playing into the hands of self-hatred or real bigotry when you do BDSM around racial identity? Aren't you afraid of being really damaged?

These are all questions I have been asked, and asked myself, ever since I realized that I had a visceral curiosity about pushing the edges of my kinky play into the most oblique corners of my psyche.

Can you really play with the terrible truths of hatred and racism and oppression and reemerge safely?

Yes. I do. I do it, albeit selectively and extremely rarely, because it is a quick slide to one of the darkest edges of my psyche, and that of my play partners. It is emotionally dangerous. Like life. And yes, I live it. And yes, I have experienced racism. But that doesn't lead me to fight, flight or fear…which are all heads of the same Cerberus.

I am curious about fucked-up edge play, so I "go there."

Every pervert has touchstones in their lives, moments where something clicked for them, and they realized they weren't like all of the other rabbits in the warren. Unsurprisingly, I have many. But the moment I remember as being one of the most jarring was the time I was sitting with my mother and watching "Roots" as it unfolded in all of its serialized glory. This was an amazing event, and I was glad to see the stories of people from whom I'd descended portrayed on television. And as a child actor, "Roots" was a bonanza for me: several commercials in which I appeared were running throughout the time slot. They knew millions of Black Americans were glued to their televisions, and we'd just stated to emerge as a marketable demographic.

The moment of difficulty came when I began thinking, objectively, about slavery. I wondered if, possibly…just maybe…it wouldn't be so bad if your master was…nice. And maybe he gave you an okay bed to sleep in, and some decent food. And if he was handsome, then that would be kind of neat, too! I started to wonder who I might like to have as my master, if I had one. I mean maybe Chuck Connors wasn't someone I wanted as *my* master, but Captain Kirk…yeah, that would be great!

I asked my mom whether or not there were ever masters who were nice to their slaves. It made sense to me that there had to be. My mom was at first puzzled, then increasingly baffled, by my line of questioning. And so of course I dropped it.

It was clear to me I was asking questions that didn't even have any business being asked, and I felt horrible for even doubting the unilateral evil of slavery.

Of course, I was ignorant of "consensual slavery." And my idea of "kinky stuff" was whispered jokes about spanking and the gay men who I'd see in the West Village in chaps and leather.

It wasn't until I had a lover with an intensely brutal sensuality and a natural capacity to inspire me to submit, to strive to please him in any way I possibly could, that it dawned on me that my kink wasn't just a passing fancy. James was a musician, from the U.K., and even after our fast-and-furious affair ended, we kept in touch when his touring schedule took him away from the West Coast. Nothing like good old phone sex to keep the torch I carried for him burning.

One long intercontinental telephone conversation and mutual masturbation session devolved and shifted into a speculation of how beautiful my skin would look covered in whip marks.

"What, like Kunta fucking Kinte? No thanks, man. I'll pass on that 'Roots' shit."

He laughed. "You'd make am absolutely shite slave anyway."

I bristled in mock indignation. "What are you trying to say? I would make an awesome slave!" I laughed.

"*No.* You would not. You'd be in the kitchen pulling down the china and upsetting the bloody tea cart so that you'd get your black ass beaten and shagged proper, wouldn't you?"

I paused, something shifting along the surface of my entire body. It was as though an old "me," a part I'd forgotten and yet was never there, was pulled, gasping, from the depth of my id.

"I...probably yeah..." I stammered, and laughed as I realized that I was more turned on than was feasible for phone-sex drive afterglow.

"That is kind of hot..." I whispered to him. "Maybe I'll write you a story like that...about me being your slave."

"I'd love that, baby girl," he growled.

The Admiral sat on the edge of the navy blue overstuffed ottoman, extending his foot and gesturing impatiently toward his boot. Dutifully, I knelt, pulling on the heel and toe. On the second boot, I was startled by his sudden and firm grip as he grasped my jaw. My eyes widened, and I lost my balance, sliding suddenly toward the floor. My hands hit the cold polished marble to break my fall. Yet he still held my head.

He spoke in a low tone, his voice rumbling in his chest. "Look at me." Why I was shaking, I could not say. I gazed into his eyes and was trapped as surely as the sparrow in the cobra's reptilian stare. For an eternity, he said nothing. Finally, I could not look at him anymore and I lowered my gaze. He laughed, and tightened his grip on my throat.

"Be certain, I will discuss with your Master my desire to have you serve me, and me alone. You will be my handmaid for the duration of my sojourn here. You will obey me unconditionally while I am here, precious...I will have to retrain you myself, and that will take some time. I have little of that now, however." As he spoke, he undid the hooks of his breeches. I was confused, and then horrified, to see him remove his male part right then and there. I had never seen one so closely before. Part of my mind shook in terror. Yet I was unable to look away. The Admiral seemed to sense this.

"Tell me, Molly, have you not been properly...ah...introduced?"

My mouth was dry. I could only whisper. "No, sir."

I could not take my gaze from his hand wrapped around the enormous shaft thrusting aggressively from his lap. The tip was moist and split at the end and I was sickened. As I tried to back away, the hand on my throat deftly slid around to the back of my neck, forcing my face closer to it.

"You will kiss it, my girl." I shook violently and threw myself backward, away from him. Momentarily escaping his grip, I slid farther on the floor, gasping. I dared not shout. I did not want to be beaten. I could not fathom why this refined man would demand such an awful and perverted thing of me.

The Admiral startled, but recovered quickly and was upon me in a second. That icy smile was back upon his face. In a flash, he had my back pressed to the cold floor, straddling me across the chest, pinning my arms to my sides, one calloused hand again on my neck. He was breathing heavily, despite the fact that he had hardly exerted himself. His male part was now mere inches from my face, and I turned away. In the corner of my vision, I saw a flash, and suddenly the left side of my face stung. Then he slapped the right. I had rarely ever been struck, and the effect was electric. As my mouth fell open in protest, he pushed his thumb between my teeth. I considered biting, as hard as I could, but I thought it better to wait.

"That was quite amusing, my dear. Now. Back to our lesson."

He took his hand, wrapped it about his privates, and resumed his hypnotic stroking. I could not look away.

"Open your mouth, Molly. If you are so foolish to believe that a bite from those strong little teeth will save you, do not. You will take my cock into your mouth for me, and pass your tongue around it until I tell you otherwise. Is that clear?" I could only blink at him. His face darkened with impending anger. "I am growing impatient, little Molly. Do not feign ignorance…" I shook my head in a panic, tears welling to my eyes and sliding down my cheeks and into my ears. "Am I to believe you are not in the habit of servicing your Masters properly, then?"

I had started to understand his meaning. I shook my head, slowly.

"Have you never even been properly fucked?"

I shuddered at the ugliness of that word. I could not reconcile my terror and indignation with a vaguely shamed sense that, somehow, I had fallen short.

I shook my head again. As fresh tears ran down my face, I was amazed to see him throw back his head, roaring with laughter.

"By Jove! This is more delightful than I could have hoped for." Leaning down, he took my face in his hands. I was weeping openly now, beyond caring. He placed his finger firmly against my lips, his chilly smile quelling my sobs. He leaned closer, and I felt his breath hot upon my skin. I shook violently as I felt the broad, firm sweep of his tongue caressing my cheek, wet with tears, and licking them away. I could not catch my breath. I was suddenly aware of his cock pressed hard and hot against my belly. I looked into his eyes and saw him watching me closely. He released me, and I knelt up before him.

The Admiral stood and walked over to the stool. He fastened his breeches, with some difficulty. Sitting on the ottoman once more, he pulled on his heavy boots. I moved to stand, and in an instant, he was before me again, his enormous fingers pressed into my throat. I looked up, confused. "In my presence, my darling child, you will not move unless I order you, or you have requested my permission, and you will address me as your Master." He pulled a heavy gold watch out of his waistcoat pocket, flipped open the catch, and sighed. "I shall have to begin properly after tea."

He started away from me, paused, and turned back, grasping me about my waist. Without warning, he lifted me to my feet and threw me, facedown, onto the huge bed. I was not accustomed to such a pleasant and yielding surface. Momentarily forgetting my fear, I marveled at the softness. I had little time to relish this as I found my mouth quickly and firmly gagged. The Admiral's cravat was secured about my head. He turned me on my back, one hand tightly pressing my wrists against the coverlet. In one fluid motion, he pulled up my dress and pulled down my underthings, tossing them to the floor.

Immediately, he was upon the bed, kneeling beside me, and I felt his hand groping upward. Unthinkingly, I screamed, but my cries were effectively muzzled by the tie. He laughed at my futile struggles as his hand reached higher and up to the cleft between my legs. I twisted violently, but only succeeded in aiding him, as his fingers grasped me firmly. I felt him touch me, gently, and I was shocked into stillness. A quivering seizure struck my belly, and I could only shrink back into the bed as he softly chuckled and stroked me more firmly. My eyes slid halfway closed involuntarily, and I found it difficult to draw a steady breath. He tried to push his thick fingers farther into me, and reached a tight resistance. Under his breath, he murmured, "By Christ, the little bitch wasn't lying…" He grinned ferociously at me, and I cowered away, confused. I felt horribly ashamed and yet…as he pulled his hand away, my hips lifted ever so slightly toward him. Mortified, I hoped he had not noticed, but it was too late. He displayed that terrifying smile again. He grasped between my legs, and leaned his face to my ear. I could feel the roughness of his cheek as it grazed mine. His hand relinquished not its possessive grip.

"This cunt is mine. Is that clear?"

Cunt. I had never heard that word: repulsive, yet strangely compelling. I nodded.

"May I rely on your silence, should I remove this binding?"

I nodded once more.

"Splendid." He undid the tie, and I licked my parched lips. His smile broadened and warmed. In a flash he rose, crossed to the armoire and shrugged on his jacket, looking for all the world as though he had just come from a relaxing stroll.

"Sir."

"Yes, Molly."

"Sir…I…what shall I…" I was not at all sure of what to do. I paused.

"Good girl. You learn quickly. For this afternoon, you will serve at tea. I shall begin your training later this evening. Come along now."

"Yes, sir." I stood and went to retrieve my crumpled underthings from the floor. Quick and silent, the Admiral was at my side. Afraid, I backed away, but he only laughed, pulling them out of my hand.

"Molly."

"Yes, sir."

"Never wear these again. I want to know that I have access to my cunt at all times." Reaching between my legs, his hand unerringly found my moist inner place.

I shuddered. He smiled.

"Is this understood?" At once repelled and excited, I whispered, "Yes, sir."

"I did not hear you, my dearest."

I raised my voice. "Yes, sir."

"Brilliant. Now, tea time. I'm famished."

My first tentative steps in the BDSM community were back in 1996 and consisted of a year of research, reading, online perving. When I worked up the nerve to attend real-time events, I would frequently be the only Black person there, and often the only nonwhite person. I noted this, but since I had little choice if I wanted to explore the fantasy that weighed on my heart more heavily every day, I had to work with what I had. My first relationship was with a dominant who was averse to any play that smacked of racism. The irony was that, willy-nilly, he was a white man tying up and whipping and flogging and tormenting a Black woman.

I had a woman, white, approach me not too long ago and relate to me that she'd seen my playing, many years ago, and that it was "very difficult!" for her to watch. Specifically, to watch a white man beating and torturing a Black woman. "I wish someone could have warned me! That is a pretty intense thing to see when you walk into a playspace."

I sighed. "You know what's funny? That wasn't a race-play scene. That man didn't do race play. What you saw was the man to whom I was in service playing with me. What you perceived was a race-play scene. I can't warn you about your own perceptions."

And so it goes.

I do "race play" whether or not I want to. I have had white tops decline to play with me because they were squicked by the idea of playing with a Black person. White guilt? Oh, it lives and thrives here in the San Francisco Bay Area! But this presents a quandary. If there are so few people of color in the scene, and a segment of the community feels bad about beating me, who the hell am I supposed to play with?

Eventually, I did find partners who were willing to push that boundary with me, often with explosive results. The toughest aspect of playing in this dark and turbulent dimension wasn't even the play itself; it was the fury with which some people reacted to even the topic of race-based play being raised. On several BDSM-focused discussion groups, my writings on my play drew ire, fire and all manner of wrath. I had other Black people labeling me a "self-hating Black woman," a "traitor to the race," "deeply disturbed and in need of serious counseling," and "unfit to be in the community." Some have even gone so far as to indicate that they would lash out violently if they were ever to be in the proximity of anyone engaging in this type of play.

That isn't too sexy. I like my violence consensual.

It took me a while to digest this vitriol. I lost friends, was removed from several social groups, uninvited from some events.

But I also had people, more and more often, writing me privately, telling me they'd had similar fantasies. Other Black people. Jewish people who have had fantasies of Nazi interrogations. People of Japanese descent who wonder what an internment camp scene might feel like. Native Americans mulling the idea of a mock "scalping" of a captured white soldier.

It wasn't just me.

Therefore, dialogue was needed. And I was willing to initiate it.

Within the BDSM community, there are often classes and seminars that folks attend to expand their skill set, or to just investigate something new and curious to them. In my case, I have about a dozen classes I love teaching, and the list expands. But one of the things that never seems to wane is folk's desire to discuss the hard stuff. Play that is race based. Play that burns away the niceties of political correctness. Play that is hard. Brutal real.

Playing with an assumed role in BDSM is difficult for some, easy for others. Playing a role that incorporates part of who you really are brings it closer to home. Playing with real-time fears and hatreds is hot for precisely the same reason it is risky: danger. Danger of slipping into a bad headspace. Danger of believing that your top really is a racist. Danger of believing that your bottom really is your inferior and has no intrinsic value, is less than human, because of their race.

But don't we all?

Aren't we all walking that day to day?

I have had Black people tell me they thought it was ridiculous that I did this kind of play, and that they never would because, "I live it, why would I need to play it?"

Because we live pain. For me, BDSM is about transcendence. There is nothing as fierce as the pride I have in myself after a scene in which I have weathered the physical abuse, as well as the emotional slings and arrows of my partner, and endured.

This despite my fear that I am unleashing a monstrous army of thoughtless white people now skulking within the dungeons of America, looking for the next available "minority" to thoughtlessly degrade. Quite the opposite seems to be the case. I am almost never approached by white folks interested in specifically engaging in this type of play with me. More often than not, I am politely turned down when I ask friends if they would be interested in playing with me in that way. Don't even get me started on how impossible it is to find someone to agree to participate as a top in a demo for one of my classes on race play.

The first time I did a race-based class for a kink event my "demo top" was a dear friend who is of Mexican descent. I felt it was necessary to awaken people to the possibilities of this type of play. He played the indignant homeboy—'do rag, cap to the back, baggy pants, a big chain—who pulled a knife on me because he didn't like the way I was looking at him. I played the snotty Black woman looking down her nose at the wetback thug. And no one knew really what to think. Which was fantastic.

Subsequently, I taught a class with a friend with whom I had played on this edge quite a few times. He was beyond worrying about being perceived as a bigot, and therefore had no trouble doing the scene.

I did a demo with him that involved a job interview gone terribly, terribly wrong, an HR nightmare where, as part of the interview query, I was asked if I would be bringing the requisite fried chicken and watermelon to the company picnic, were I hired. The interview, of course, proceeded to a humiliating climax wherein I was made to debase myself for his amusement because, of course, "Your people are good at shucking and jiving, right?"

In the case of this demo, I was playing with someone I knew very well. There was then a lag of a couple of years where I was dating a guy who, though quite kinky in his own right, was not interested in the public BDSM scene. He was white, and interestingly, he had no trouble at all with the "pillow talk" being of a very racially charged nature. He was also a Southerner, so the traces of drawl that inflected his speech always drove me to distraction. It is enticing to have your lover make you beg for his cock. For me, the rough sex was even hotter and dirtier with the added facet of "wrongness." No one need know that I was, late at night in the closed bedroom, his "slutty black whore" choking down his "huge white cock." Even as part of me was furious at the blatant wickedness, I would orgasm just from having his cock in my mouth and listening to the stream of invective with which he abused me as he used me for his pleasure.

That relationship had an organic component to the play, and after it ended, I had a long lag where I was still teaching classes, but rarely did the classes have demos, because I had so few people with whom I was comfortable doing that type of play.

Usually I prefer, even insist on being the instigator of racially charged play. I need to be able to look, objectively, at the top in question and see how I feel about them as a person, how they are within the community, if I like them and can see myself forming a friendship. Without this knowledge, I can't begin to think about exploring very dark edge play. Someone who approaches me outright will immediately put me into a defensive mode. I'll always wonder if the reason they asked me was because they really are a closeted racist and I am a convenient outlet.

I was slated to teach a class on race play in Chicago, and I was not planning on having a demo for the class. It was a city mostly unknown to me, and I'd have none of the people who I might feel comfortable scening with in attendance. I was surprised when a new acquaintance of mine, also a presenter in the BDSM and leather community, offered to help by acting as demo top for this presentation. I knew Gray (aka Graydancer) well enough that my hackles weren't raised, but I was curious as to what inspired him to put himself out there in that manner.

"I offered to help with Mollena's race-play workshop for a variety of reasons, none of which was that I enjoy playing with racial stereotypes," said Graydancer. "It's not something I've ever had an interest in, any more than medical play or age play. The reasons were more selfish than that—wanting to see Mollena, wanting to expand my own skills as a 'demo top,' wanting to go visit my old stomping grounds in Chicago. But there was definitely a tinge of edge play to the material itself, a kind of challenge to my own comfort zone, a question of 'Are you really a good enough top to be able to go there, and not just make it work, but make it hot?' Going into the workshop was very much like the feeling you get at the top of a ski hill you've never tried, or as you approach the edge of the high-diving board. Am I really going to do this?"

Since he had no experience in this type of play, I mustered up the courage to send to him the story I'd started writing for James all those years ago, a segment of which you just read. We did some basic negotiation, and that was pretty much it. This was a real cliff dive, as he was as much at risk as I was in this scene: I wasn't that worried about how far I might go, or about negative feedback. I've been down that road before. But I knew it could possibly be dodgy for Gray, so I made it clear to the class that not only was it the first time I was doing this type of scene (an explicitly Antebellum South–style plantation scene) but also it was his maiden flight into this turbulent air.

I was surprised by the immediate submissive headspace I hit in this scene, but in retrospect, it made total sense. Gray had been privy to a fantasy that had lain, pristine, for over a decade. In my head there were all of the emotional trips and triggers that would be critical to making the scene hot. I wondered if I would be aroused or disgusted with myself for permitting this scene to breathe into life, but after the opening salvo, and as my clothes were sliced and ripped from me in preparation for punishment by this rather brutal and sadistic "slave trader," there was no doubt that I was not only turned on but completely in tune with this fantasy. As the bottom, I am able to roll with the flow of the scene, but the top is the one who has to keep things afloat. They have to do the steering, the pushing. That was Gray's job.

"While doing it, there wasn't much thought involved," Graydancer said. "No thought about the ethics or morality of it, anyway. I was in the moment, playing a character I'd plucked right out of Mollena's own fantasies, doing my best to break through her shell of self-control by hitting precise pressure points in her psyche, and doing it with as much method acting as I could muster."

It was certainly beneficial to Gray to try this type of scene with, essentially, a blueprint and an experienced bottom. Even as I was pushed over a bench so that I could be "inspected" for "usefulness" and then was found lacking, the shame I felt veered from shame at my wanting this to happen at all to shame at the "me" who was truly present in the role-play feeling shame at somehow failing to be pleasing. The framework of this dynamic provides a set, lighting, and costume for the psyche to play out the emotional drama. We already have this knowledge, this shame, this nightmare, and yes, this lust, within us. The capacity to pull it out and make it arousing is nothing short of miraculous.

I'd joked with Gray that he would probably have people asking him how the scene was for him afterward, because of the relative scarcity of whites who do this type of play. Everyone wants to know how it feels to be "the oppressor" in these scenes, and this is a unique opportunity for them.

I'd left the demo area for a moment to put on some clothes after the scene, and catch my breath. As I returned to the classroom, I heard a Black woman who was in the class participating in the discussion. "I really wanted to jump in there and help you a few times," she was saying. I turned to her, a bit bleary but grateful for the support. It is scary up there! As I started to speak, she waved me off. "No, no, not you. Gray. He was being way too nice to you."

Nonplussed, I turned to Gray. "There you go! Always leave 'em wanting more."

He was surprised by the responses as well. "We came to the end of the scene, and that was when it got weird. People were concerned, people wanted to make sure everything was okay with *me*, not Mollena, who had been beaten, terrorized, and literally dehumanized. No, the questions were coming from people—regardless of skin color—who wanted to make sure I was okay, that my psyche had not been bruised. In fact, when I travel through the Midwest I will still get people who come up to me and express appreciation for the demo. I've never heard one negative comment."

That was an added flavor of humiliation, unexpected even for me, and, in the way that the pain can be pleasurable, yet another shove down the slope of erotic humiliation.

Humiliation is a delicate balancing act. The person laying on the abuse has to remain focused, and watch themselves and their bottom for signs of the scene veering off course. There is a very likely possibility that something you say will push a button, and some reaction—rage, fear, terror, despair—will rear its head and start flailing about, thrashing in its pain and potentially dragging the scene to a destructive place.

For me, humiliation is a broad-brush full-bore way for me to feel the worst of how I feel about myself, give it away to someone, and have them hold it.

Once someone else holds it up for me, mirrors it back, shows me the depth of my own feelings, my self-deprecation, I can see it for what it is.

And then they let it go.

And then, they come back, and love me for who I *truly* am.

And then, sometimes just for a second, but usually for much

longer, I feel immensely powerful. Present. Whole.

Add to this mix the humiliation of years of racism, oppression, the struggle for identity. Add to this living in a country built by your ancestors and one where, in your parents' memory, your ancestors were living in segregation.

Imagine, instead of covering up that scar, that wound, pulling it open, letting that suppurating pain see the light of day, bare, open and painful, but able to breathe, to heal, and so find peace in surviving it.

I go there because I am that much more powerful for taking that which I cannot control and shaping it into something I *can* control, and learning from this.

And the next time someone mutters an epithet under their breath, or I'm followed in a store by security, or get "That Look" when walking into a restaurant, I can take a deep breath, focus my energies, and do battle with that monster as I see fit.

Because I have tamed the dragon, and now we play.

Remembering Pubic Hair
Paul Krassner

Okay, call me old-fashioned, but I still like pubic hair. Internet porn sites now present several choices—completely shaved, vertical landing strips that look like exclamation points, heart shaped, the Charlie Chaplin with just a little patch above the clitoris, and a tiny triangle that serves as an arrow *pointing* to the clit—yet, for pubic follicles one has to search the Web for "hairy" sites that are considered as "specialty," "kinky" or "fetish."

Retired porn stars have commented on this phenomenon. Gina Rome, retired after six years, shaved every day. "It was part of getting ready for work." When she switched from acting to film editing, she stopped shaving and let her pubic hair grow out. "Shaving was work. I don't have to do it anymore, so I don't." And Kelly Nichols says, "I was a *Penthouse* model in the early 1980s, and I posed with a full bush. No one in adult entertainment shaved back then. Now everybody does."

Although Martha Stewart is back on TV, you can be sure that she'll never give any suggestions on what to do about those big red razor bumps that result from shaving your vagina, so here's a helpful hint I'd like to pass along—they can be largely eliminated with, of all things, Visine eyedrops.

The porn industry has played an important part in shaping pubic styles. Jordan Stein writes in an article titled "Has Porn Gone Mainstream?": "Consider the near icon status the female porn star has achieved. She is so mainstream that even good girls are imitating her various styles of undress, disappearing hair and all. Porn chic? You bet."

However, Julia Baird writes in *Celebrity Porn*: "The idea that the fashion industry can strip, then exhibit women in the name of 'porn chic' is a bit silly, frankly. But, 'flesh is the new fabric' could be the new catchcry. Americans call their bush George W. It's fashionable—the curious fact is that it is fueled by the porn aesthetic that celebrities love to love."

Among Hollywood actresses, Gwyneth Paltrow and Kirstie Alley have both admitted favoring Brazilian wax jobs, where most of their pubic hair is removed, leaving a small tuft that remains hidden under a thong bikini. Sarah Jessica Parker's character, Carrie Bradshaw, had her pubic hair removed during the third season of "Sex and the City." Presumably, it's now in the Smithsonian Museum along with Archie Bunker's chair and the Fonz's jacket.

On ABC's "Women's Murder Club," a medical examiner directs her gaze to the crotch of a female corpse and says, "That's not your mama's bikini wax." On "The View," Joy Behar said, "No pubic hair creates a wind tunnel." And in a hysterical episode of HBO's dark comedy series, "Curb Your Enthusiasm," former "Seinfeld" producer Larry David performed oral sex on his wife, and in the process he sort of swallowed one of her pubic

Go Thin or Bust: How Berkeley's Mayer Laboratories Won the Battle of the Thin Condoms
Rachel Swan

A 2005 commercial for Kimono condoms speaks volumes about the company's self-image. In the ad, a woman sits at a poker table with four men. The setup is swank: chandelier light reflects from the walls, glass tumblers litter the table, smooth jazz plays in the background. When the woman runs out of dough, she wagers a single Kimono condom, and another player sees her bet with all his remaining chips. It's a fitting analogy for a company that presents itself both as an underdog, and a producer of high-end condoms. Consider the tagline: "Kimono. When the Stakes Are High."

In a market dominated by Trojan and Durex, where images of male virility are the norm, Berkeley-based Kimono has created a brand identity that's an anathema to the competition. Launched twenty-one years ago by Mayer Laboratories, a company founded by longtime birth-control advocate David Mayer, Kimono is the condom industry's answer to couture. It's a sleek, elegant Japanese import with a pretty patina—packages are designed with cranes, koi and other Japanese imagery—and a price about 15 to 20 percent higher than most other brands.

"Kimono as a name is a Japanese silk robe," said Mayer at his office in downtown Berkeley. "But that was all part of our marketing when we started…to try to communicate more that condoms can be silky and thin and sheer and elegant—and something that women might approach as a kimono versus as a Trojan."

Mayer lowered his voice disparagingly on the word "Trojan," the U.S. industry's dominant brand, which he considers to be the Exxon-Mobil of condoms. He's repelled by the military imagery bound up in the Trojan name and the phallic metaphors in its advertising language. (After all, Trojan's perennially popular Trojan Magnum XL just happens to share its name with the handgun used in *Dirty Harry*.) "I just think they're marketed more toward men," Mayer said of Trojan and other industry big boys like Durex and LifeStyles. "You know, race cars, high-performance sex. Women aren't interested in that, but it tends to hit a different demo."

Indeed, the American condom industry is anything but demure. In fact, it's often quite cutthroat. Companies routinely appropriate one another's terminology and brand identities. They send litigious letters to one another and race to beat one another to the trademark office.

Mayer and Kimono have gone against the grain in marketing their products, basing their brand identity on the apparently radical notion that there are other ways to market condoms besides affirming the penis size of the buyer. Instead, Kimono markets its condoms as being so thin and silky that they're practically not there. In short, the company appeals not only to women, but also to a different side of male vanity—the squeamish impulses that make many guys resistant to using a condom in the first place.

Kimono may look like a sensitive girly-mon in the condom world, but it's allowed Mayer to grow his business by cultivating a market that all the big boys now seem interested in infiltrating. Ironically, Mayer did this by claiming to sell the country's thinnest condoms—a concept that seems to be at cross purposes with the very function of condoms, which is to provide reliable protection from pregnancy and sexually transmitted diseases without breaking.

Now, it seems like the whole condom industry is fighting over who makes the least-condom-like condom.

Mayer Laboratories is located in a pristine downtown Berkeley office complex, home to insurance salesmen, lawyers and a popular local artist who illustrates *New Yorker* covers. The place is bright and well-ventilated, and a pebble garden in the foyer could have been transplanted from any high-end department store in Union Square. The lab looks like any other office space. There aren't any Willy Wonka-type condom machines spitting colored disks of latex onto a conveyor belt; nor are there any seedy adult ads on the walls. Rather, it's antiseptic, with cubicles and a large conference room in the back where, on a recent Tuesday afternoon, Mayer laid out his whole arsenal of products.

Arrayed on the long table were six packages of condoms from Mayer's line Kimono, along with packages of other Mayer products such as Aqua Lube, Digitex gloves, and the fc female condom. In the condom world, these are all considered to be high-end designer products: more elegant, more expensive, and more feminine than the average Trojan or Durex contraceptive. For Mayer, they hold sentimental value, symbolizing his effort to carve out a distinctive brand identity that could sustain a small Berkeley condom-maker. They also illustrate Mayer's seemingly counterintuitive quest to popularize the world's thinnest condom.

Few people in the world can boast a condom history as long as that of David Mayer. In 1978, he launched National Condom Week as a freshman at UC Berkeley, spent several years working in teen programs in the Contra Costa County Health Department, and traveled to Haiti in 1984 to promote public health and family planning. Mayer describes himself as having a history of "male involvement in family planning," and says that even if he had never spawned his own condom line, his impact would still be felt in the contraceptive world. The American Social Health Association still plans National Condom Week events every year (although after thirty years, Mayer said it has kind of gone the way of Valentine's Day).

When Mayer launched Kimono in 1987, the AIDS epidemic had generated a surge in consumer demand, and companies just needed to fill the pipeline. By then, most condom companies had product lines with contoured tips, ribs, studs, and splashy colors. But Mayer thought he knew another type of aesthetic that could get people to buy more condoms.

From his company's inception, Mayer sought out Japanese manufacturers. His reasoning was that Japan had higher quality standards and looser restrictions on condom thickness. Because Japan didn't legalize oral contraceptives until 1999, its market for other forms of birth control was quite advanced. Mayer said Kimono's reliance on more-advanced Japanese condom-making technology helped his company push up against the U.S. Food and Drug Administration's .03 millimeter (or 30 micron) minimum-thickness limit. Mayer conceptualized his brand accordingly.

Even before Kimono began cultivating the super-thin market, competitors paid close attention to its products. In 1988 Mayer Laboratories introduced the Kimono Maxx, a special plus-sized condom with extra head room (2.34 inches in diameter) and an additional .2 inches of length. Roughly seven months later, Trojan unleashed the Magnum XL, an 8.5-inch "King of the Big Boys" that has become the gold standard for large-sized condoms (given that it's name-checked in rap songs and worthy of its own Wikipedia definition).

Not to be outdone, Kimono shifted its focus to thinness and delicacy. In 1992 it came out with the Kimono MicroThin, which the company claims is 20 percent thinner than the original Kimono. For sixteen years, Kimono has claimed that MicroThin is the thinnest condom sold in the United States. According to Mayer, regular Kimonos—at 55 microns of thickness—were already 20 percent thinner than most other brands. The new MicroThins measured 49 microns, Mayer said, "So now we are really ahead of our competition offering that really thin, sheer experience for users."

The product was groundbreaking, according to one local retailer. "I do believe they were the first people to bring in ultra-thin condoms that were strong and comfortable, but offered the maximum sensation that allowed people to feel like they weren't wearing anything at all," said Coyote Days, senior buyer at the adult store Good Vibrations, which has carried Kimono for well over ten years. "They're a premium line; they have different contours and different sizes. A piece of their own marketing was that they were Japanese-made, and that stood for a high quality."

Before Kimono hit the market, Days said, there wasn't much incentive for big companies like Trojan (now eighty-eight years old) or Durex (now ninety-three years old) to enlarge their brands or expand their customer base. But slowly that's changing. "It's 'the way we've always done it' versus 'the way we're gonna do it now,'" Days said. "Someone comes in with a new idea, a strong brand, and something you don't have, you're gonna feel a little threatened and you're gonna step up to the challenge."

And step up they did. Although Mayer says it took his competitors several years to acquire the ability to produce super-thin condoms (which they too accomplished by sourcing from Japan), they began appropriating his company's language right away—even for condoms whose thinness he claims is questionable.

"Now it's 'Sensi-Thin,'" said Mayer, referring to the new thin condom category from Durex, "but before that they had 'Ultra Sensitive,' 'Extra Sensitive.' Those would be the terms they would use, but it would more or less be the same condom.... And then Trojan came out with a line called 'Ultra Thin.' They came out this year with 'Thintensity.' And then 'Magnum Thin.'"

In fact, there's no shortage of "thin," "sensitive," or Japanese-styled condoms on the market. Visit the popular Web retailer RipnRoll.com and you'll find—in addition to the aforementioned Trojan and Durex products—Lifestyles Skyn condoms, Lifestyles Ultra Thin, Paradise Super Sensitive, Intellx spiral-shaped Inspiral, and Okamoto's Beyond Seven with aloe (another Japanese import).

Mayer recently began appending a bar graph to Kimono packages claiming that even its regular Kimono Thin condoms are as thin as Durex Extra Sensitive and thinner than Lifestyles Ultra Thins. And Kimono claims that its MicroThin beats everyone—including the super-stretchy Trojan Ultra Thin condoms—by several microns.

"We've been calling ourselves 'Microthin' since the beginning, and now one of our other competitors, Trojan, they came out and started using the 'Microthin' for their condoms," said Mayer. "Now we're having to look at, do we need to take them to task?" Mayer says Trojan appropriated the "Microthin" label last year, right around the time its "Thintensity" condom line hit drugstore shelves. The company also took Kimono's tack of manufacturing the Microthin condoms in Japan. "They went to one of our competitors," he said, bitterly. Mayer concedes, however, that Kimono never got around to trademarking the term Microthin until April of 2008, sixteen years after it first started using the phrase.

Mayer says the word "microthin" appeared on Trojan Ultra Thin packages in 2007, which advertised the new Ultra Thin condoms as being "made with 'microthin technology.'" "In some ways it was a concession," said Mayer, alluding to the use of his brand name to describe a competitor's product. Although these words no longer show up on Trojan's website, their occurrence in consumer product forums suggests that Trojan did indeed use them. But then, "micro" is a ubiquitous adjective, recycled again on a package of Trojan Supra "Microsheer" Polyurethane Ultra Thin Lubricated Premium condoms.

Meanwhile, a couple months ago, one of Mayer's customers informed him of some new marketing material from Durex, which advertised its new "Sensi-Thin" condom as "the thinnest in the world." When the product hit stores a month later, Mayer got a pack and read the marketing claim, which he said was specious. Mayer said Durex alleged that the Kimono MicroThin was 59 microns thick, while falsely advertising itself as being 45 microns thick. Not true, said Mayer, who insisted that MicroThin had always stuck with its official 49 micron measurement. He was incensed, to say the least.

"We went and tested several boxes of their product. They had this interesting language that claimed they were the thinnest condom in the world…based on what they called the mass method of measurement." According to Mayer, this measurement standard is seldom used by manufacturers. "What it is, you take your weight of your condom, divide it by your length of your condom, divide it by some other things, and it comes out with a calculated thickness."

So Mayer measured the Kimonos against the "Sensi-Thins," using both the Durex method and his own, which takes the thickness of the condom walls at three points using a micrometer caliper (an instrument accurate enough to measure the width of a single hair). In both cases, he claims, Durex's claims were wrong. Mayer wrote a letter to Bill Siegel, the president of Durex, asking him to cease and desist. Mayer said Siegel replied with a promise to rescind the "world's thinnest condom" slogan, although he defended Durex's data. (In fact, Sensi-Thins are still advertised as "the thinnest latex condom in the world" on several websites.)

Durex representatives did not respond to repeated requests for comment. Asked to comment for this story, Siegel of Durex replied with this canned statement: "As the world's number one condom brand, Durex® leads the way in research, innovation, and technology which allows us to offer a wide range of high quality condom options for consumers all over the world. We do not feel it's appropriate to discuss competitors in the media and are therefore not in a position to respond further to your inquiries."

In any case, shortly after his exchange with Siegel, Mayer sent a press release advertising this tit-for-tat as a "David vs. Goliath story." An attached picture showed the Durex Sensi-Thins package with the slogan "World's THINNEST latex condom!" circled and crossed out.

For Mayer it was a small victory.

Condom advertising is more visible today than ever before, and it's not uncommon to turn on a Top 40 radio station these days and hear one of the new ads for Durex, Trojan or Lifestyles.

Among the far more adventurous Web commercials are a Trojan Olympic sport called "pelvic power lifting" and the alleged "president" of Durex slamming his wang with a car door.

But despite the macho swagger of ads such as these, the industry's commercial imagery has softened and even grown a little more sophisticated over three decades, which might be related to the gradual feminization of condoms. Clearly, there's an overwhelming interest in thin condoms. Days of Good Vibrations says it's no accident. "Both women and men buy them in massive amounts. We sell tens of thousands of Kimonos a year, and of the super-thin condoms in general."

Trojan spokesperson Nyla Saleh said the competition to sell America's thinnest condom is driven by consumer demand. "People want something that's gonna have more of a natural feel, and Ultra Thin condoms are able to provide a lot of consumers with that," she said in a phone interview. "We also have very extensive focus groups that we have for each product. We take into huge account consumer reactions and personal testimonials to all of our products."

But is "thin" really what consumers are looking for, or are companies just rebranding their existing products? A random survey of current and former condom buyers suggested that men and women have a wide range of reasons for buying a particular brand of condom.

Some consumers unequivocally champion thinness. In an online discussion entitled, "What's the thinnest, least 'intrusive' condom on the market?" at the website MetaFilter, one anonymous commenter described the thinking of many condom buyers. "I'm pretty tired of my penis being encased in what feels like an inch of rubber. I'm not concerned about STDs because I'm in a monogamous relationship and we've both recently had

STD panels, but I'd really prefer not to have little anonymouses around. Any suggestions on really super-thin or super, um, sensation-transferring condoms?"

Kimono condoms are generally conceded to be desirable by consumers interested in thin condoms. The web retailer SpicyGear.com named Kimono MicroThins the "thinnest latex condoms made," and competitor CondomUSA is similarly enthusiastic: "Japanese condoms are our favorite because they are thinner and feel better. We vote Kimono MicroThin as our Editor Choice because we believe it is one of the best and thinnest condoms in the market. It surprises us by its thinness and quality. Because it is so thin, it reduces the 'rubber' feeling and feels like nothing at all."

"Big J," who reviewed Kimono MicroThins on the Walgreens website, wrote: "This is the best condom ever. It's like wearing nothing at all."

Other people agreed with Mayer, albeit with reservations: "The problem is if you're doing anal sex, they're less sturdy," said "Chaz." "But you can definitely feel more."

But many seemed unimpressed with claims about which brand is thinner.

"Sure, thicker condoms reduce the physical sensation of sex," said Steve, who described himself as a lifelong Trojan buyer. "But is a little less sensation really a bad thing? When I buy a condom, I'm thinking about babies and disease. If the condom also happens to slow things down a bit, hey, that's fine by me."

Joe, a long-time Trojan user, said thinness doesn't necessarily seal the deal for everyone. He suspects that if some company made a thick condom and promised it would make you last longer, a lot of consumers would probably go for it. "There are people who would make that decision, yes, definitely," he said.

"I mean think about it. Guys buy condoms for two reasons. One, random hookup; they're just hittin' it, quittin' it. Or, two, there's people who buy condoms because they're with a partner and it helps them last longer." Joe goes for Trojan because of brand allegiance—it's been burned into his brain, "like Kleenex."

Tiffany said it might behoove these companies to advertise a super-thick condom, specifically targeting people who never get laid, and don't want to bust the moment it finally happens. She says she knows several people who would fit this consumer demographic: "They got (condoms) in their shoe, their sock, their back pocket. Probably wearing one at all times."

Kevin said, "The idea of a thin condom, it makes me nervous. It's a little tiny piece of rubber. You're gonna make it thinner? That freaks me out."

Some of Kimono's competitors make the same argument. "The thinner the condoms are, logically the more likely they are to break," said Brian Osterberg, president of condom-maker Intellx, whose said his company's shaped contraceptives represent "a new milestone" in condom-making. "There's two trains of thought here: Super-thin so that you feel through the latex, or a normal condom with oversized shapes that creates the ridges and folds, and that's what creates the friction. We turned upside down the idea that a super-thin condom is the best."

But Mayer of Kimono disagrees—he's never had a product recall, after all. Moreover, he sees no irony in his efforts to market the least-condomy condom. "The number one reason people don't use condoms is it interrupts the moment," he said. "Number two is that it's like wearing a raincoat. If we can make something that's silky and next to nothing at all, then more people will use it. Hopefully we can increase utilization because of it."

The market has gone through many significant changes since

Kimono started making condoms in 1988. Discussion of sexuality and birth control has become more socially acceptable, information about AIDS and other STDs has increasingly come into the public eye and more and more companies are marketing directly to female consumers. "Now women are buying condoms with pride," Days explained, "because it's about securing your own sexuality and feeling like a savvy buyer of sex products."

As a result, the advertising patois has changed. A popular new Trojan commercial features a Midwestern sports bar packed with pigs and beautiful women. One of the pigs turns into a man after buying a Trojan condom from a bathroom dispenser. The slogan, which comes at the very end, seems apropos: "Evolve." Days of Good Vibrations found this ad particularly intriguing. "I thought it was really interesting that they put a spin on it that was almost female-positive," she said. "It was almost one of those 'real men drink beer' [slogans], but it was 'real men wear condoms.' I thought it was really interesting to put it like 'the evolved man uses condoms'—and definitely 'the evolved woman.'"

To Mayer, all this goes to show that the big guys are finally latching on to something he realized twenty years ago. Kimono perceived itself as being a more feminine brand than the others, which is the clear logic behind the gender analogy in Kimono's "Stakes Are High" commercial. Twenty years before Trojan's "Evolve" campaign, Mayer foresaw the importance of appealing to female consumers and going thin. "We kept showing the data that that's the growth, people want good quality, reliable, thin condoms," he said. "We keep innovating. We keep coming out with thinner, better condoms, and we take the high ground."

But as the idea of importing condoms from Asian manufacturers caught on in recent years, Kimono's strategy of making its products in Japan is no longer a major selling point, Days observes.

To top it all off, she added, Lifestyles recently came up with an innovation of its own: a latex-free super-thin condom designed for people with latex allergies. "It's fantastic," she said.

In an industry in which a small number of companies battle for supremacy and most advertising is directed at retailers rather than consumers, it's a challenge for a brand the size of Kimono to stay afloat. The recent buyout of Long's Drugs by CVS, which is based in Rhode Island, could hurt Mayer Laboratories, since it's likely the newly consolidated retailer will favor national brands over regional ones.

But Kimono keeps soldiering on with innovations of its own. The company sells a girly change purse designed to hold a stash of condoms that it calls the "Kimono Kouture Bag." And last year the company began decorating its condom boxes with animals culled from Japanese myth: The Phoenix that adorns Kimono Thin packages is said to symbolize "the union of the Yin and the Yang." The ram on Kimono Maxx is "powerful, yet graceful." Kimono's textured condom, the tiger, is "daring, vigorous and passionate." There's a painterly quality to these images, suggesting that perhaps Mayer Laboratories has a backroom staff that hand-draws each package with bamboo pens and Sakuyo paintbrushes. Granted, Mayer wasn't the first condom-maker to use animal imagery. The Intellx Dolphin, a condom with a cute mammalian snout, came out a few months ago and is now on the shelves of CVS drugstores nationwide. "It's one of their hot new items," said Osterberg, who said his company has several other new shapes forthcoming—including a bell, a baseball bat, and a condom that looks like a beer glass.

"Sex Surrogates" Put Personal Touch on Therapy
Brian Alexander

"Jane" looks to be somewhere shy of forty years old, though she's squirrelly about telling me her age. She is, as she likes to say, "unaltered," not a supermodel type. She's slightly soft, ample in a pleasing way, with brown hair and an open face. I suppose you might say she's average, but she earns part of her living in a very unaverage fashion.

Jane is a sex surrogate. Los Angeles-area therapists and counselors send male patients to Jane and then she takes off her clothes and engages in that time-proven pedagogical method of teaching by doing. In the three years she's been a surrogate, she has taught about twenty men the pleasures of the flesh.

You can be forgiven if you've never heard of sex surrogates, or thought they were more urban myth than reality. But if you can recall when backyard "spas" were called hot tubs, Peter Frampton ruled and you were traumatized by the discovery of your mom's copy of *The Joy of Sex,* you may also recall that surrogates were once the rage.

The boom started when famed sex therapy pioneers Masters and Johnson revealed they had prescribed surrogates for some of their clients. Then a lot of people decided they needed therapy, too. Having a naked surrogate touch your privates or gently encourage you to have intercourse made therapy seem far more pleasant than sitting across from a shrink talking about how your oedipal complex caused your premature ejaculation.

In the ten years between 1970 and 1980, surrogacy went from being practically unknown to pop culture fascination. In 1980, one California therapist estimated there were between 400 and 500 surrogates working in the United States.

Shrinking into the Shadows
Then, like the passenger pigeon, sex surrogates seemed to disappear. Nobody knows how many are left in the United States today, but estimates from therapists who use them say there might be forty.

The reason for the disappearance was largely, though not entirely, political. Sex therapy had a sketchy reputation when it began. Throw in the notion of using a substitute sexual partner, with its heavy payload of sniggering and the foggy legality of paying for sex, and the fledgling field was at risk of being regarded as more whoopee than therapy.

Besides, after AIDS, Viagra, the explosion of sexual information, the mainstreaming of sex therapy, surrogacy came to seem an anachronistic and somewhat embarrassing holdover from the '70s, like orange shag carpeting, maxi-skirts and men with goldfish in their platform shoes.

In an effort to provide a patina of legitimacy, one surrogate named Vena Blanchard created the International Professional Surrogates Association to train and certify sex surrogates. That helped, but not much.

"A couple of things made (surrogates) problematic for some therapists," Howard Ruppel, PhD, academic dean at the Institute for Advanced Study of Human Sexuality in San Francisco, explained. "One is the matter of respectability. If you want to get an interesting discussion going on the bulletin boards of professional groups that certify sex therapists, just put surrogate partners out there and the thing goes berserk."

According to Stephen Conley, PhD, executive director of the American Association of Sexuality Educators, Counselors and Therapists, the issue of surrogacy "just about split the AASECT board years ago. They could not get consensus. Some people were strongly in favor and some worried about legal implications." AASECT never adopted a formal policy one way or the other, but the debate itself relegated surrogacy to the shadows.

"There are people out there who do work with surrogates but they are a little below the horizon and that is unfortunate," Ruppel said.

Susan Kaye, a therapist working in Philadelphia and Austin, Texas, works with surrogates "below the horizon" for a practical reason—she can't even find certified surrogates in her areas. "I have gotten around it by working with people who are 'body workers,' people I have trained on what I want them to do with clients." "Body work," as Kaye defines it, excludes intercourse, but can include genital touching and genital massage.

"There are too few therapists trained to work with surrogates," said Marilyn Lawrence, PhD, a Beverly Hills counselor who has used surrogates for thirty-five years, "and too few surrogates trained to work with therapists."

Struggling with Legality

The rationale for surrogates is simple, according to Lawrence. While patients with a regular sex partner can do therapy "homework," single men and women, who, after all, might be single because they need sex therapy, don't have study buddies. Even a partnered man or woman trying to work out a fetish, or someone who has been raped or assaulted and can't stand being touched could use a surrogate.

As Kaye explained, "You can only sit across the desk for so long and tell them how to ride a bicycle until you have to give them the bicycle."

Still, there have been no rigorous studies testing whether using a surrogate is any better than other forms of therapy. That, and the dubious legality of the practice, keeps surrogacy on the fringe.

Lawrence regards the legal issue as a red herring. In thirty-five years, neither she nor any of the surrogates she's used have faced legal trouble, probably because most legitimate surrogates do not advertise and work only with men sent to them by mental health professionals.

Indeed, if Jane's experience is any indication, men who try to use surrogates for easy, zipless sex in exchange for cash are seriously overpaying.

"I would say, of all the clients I've worked with, I have had intercourse with two," she said.

Sometimes surrogates and patients may do nothing more than hold hands and caress. "It is misunderstood," Lawrence said. "It is not a contract for sex. It is a contract to work on a problem that requires intimacy skills."

For example, Jane, who charges $150 per hour or $225 for ninety minutes, worked with a man whose Asperger's syndrome caused him to misinterpret facial expressions. "He wanted to date and he was having difficulty making connections." She has helped victims of sexual trauma, and men with depression, erectile dysfunction and fetishes that limited sexual menus.

"My favorite clients are the forty-year-old virgins," she said. "Everybody is shocked, but there are a number of men out there who, for whatever reason, have not had many successful sexual experiences or none at all."

Exactly what Jane does varies depending on the man's needs. "I reintroduce people to their own bodies," she explained. "It is close and intimate but not necessarily sexual. For example, for people with sexual trauma, it is important for them to know they can touch and be touched and not be in jeopardy."

After every session, Jane reports back to the assigning therapist who uses the information in treating the patient. For some patients, Lawrence said, surrogacy may be the only method that works.

That's why she is campaigning for the return of sexual surrogacy. "Look," she said, "sometimes all somebody needs is literature. Sometimes they need basic sex ed, sometimes talk therapy. But sometimes people need a surrogate."

What's the Matter with Teen Sexting?
Judith Levine

A couple of weeks ago, in Greensburg, Pennsylvania, prosecutors charged six teenagers with creating, distributing, and possessing child pornography. The three girls, ages fourteen and fifteen, took nude or seminude pictures of themselves and emailed them to friends, including three boys, ages sixteen and seventeen, who are among the defendants. Police Captain George Seranko described the obscenity of the images: They "weren't just breasts," he declared. "They showed female anatomy!"

Greensburg's crime-stoppers aren't the only ones looking out for the cybersafety of America's youth. In Alabama, Connecticut, Florida, New Jersey, New York, Michigan, Ohio, Pennsylvania, Texas and Utah (at last count) minors have been arrested for "sexting," or sending or posting soft-core photo or video self-portraits. Of 1,280 teens and young adults surveyed recently by the National Campaign to Prevent Teen and Unplanned Pregnancy, one in five said they engaged in the practice—girls only slightly more than boys.

Seranko and other authorities argue that such pictures may find their way to the Internet and from there to pedophiles and other exploiters. "It's very dangerous," he opined.

How dangerous is it? Not very, suggests a major study released this month by Harvard's Berkman Center for Internet Studies. "Enhancing Child Safety and Online Technologies," the result of a yearlong investigation by a wide range of experts, concludes that "the risks minors face online are in most cases not significantly different from those they face offline, and as they get older, minors themselves contribute to some of the problems." Almost all youth who end up having sex with adults they meet online seek such assignations themselves, fully aware that the partner is older. Similarly, minors who encounter pornography online go looking for it; they tend to be older teenage boys.

But sex and predatory adults are not the biggest dangers kids face as they travel the Net. Garden-variety kid-on-kid meanness, enhanced by technology, is. "Bullying and harassment, most often by peers, are the most frequent threats that minors face, both online and offline," the report found.

Just as almost all physical and sexual abuse is perpetrated by someone a child knows intimately—the adult who eats dinner or goes to church with her—victims of cyber-bullying usually know their tormenters: other students who might sit beside them in homeroom or chemistry. Social-networking sites may be the places where kids are likely to hurt each other these days, but those sites, like the bullying, "reinforce pre-existing social relations," according to the report.

Similarly, young people who get in sexual or social trouble online tend to be those who are already at risk offline—doing poorly in school, neglected or abused at home, and/or economically impoverished. According to the Centers for Disease Control and Prevention, a child from a family whose annual income is less than $15,000 is twenty-two times more likely to suffer sexual abuse than a child whose parents earn more than $30,000.

Other new research implies that online sexual communication, no matter how much there is, isn't translating into corporeal sex, with either adults or peers. Contrary to popular media depiction of girls and boys going wilder and wilder, La Salle University sociologist and criminal-justice professor Kathleen A. Bogle has found that American teens are more conservative than their elders were at their age. Teen virginity is up and the number of sexual partners is down, she discovered. Only the rate of births to teenage girls has risen in the last few years—a result of declining contraceptive use. This may have something to do with abstinence-only education, which leaves kids reluctant or incompetent when it comes to birth control. Still, the rate of teen births compared to pregnancies always tracks the rate among adult women, and it's doing that now, too.

Like the kids finding adult sex partners in chat rooms, those who fail to protect themselves from pregnancy or sexually transmitted diseases and have their babies young tend to be otherwise at risk emotionally or socially. In other words, kids who are having a rough time in life are having a rough time in virtual life as well. Sexual or emotional harm precedes risky or harmful on- and offline behavior, rather than the other way around.

Enter the law—and the injuries of otherwise harmless teenage sexual shenanigans begin. The effects of the ever-stricter sex-crimes laws, which punish ever-younger offenders, are tragic for juveniles. A child pornography conviction—which could come from sending a racy photo of yourself or receiving said photo from a girlfriend or boyfriend—carries far heavier penalties than most hands-on sexual offenses. Even if a juvenile sees no lock-up time, he or she will be forced to register as a sex offender for ten years or more. The federal Adam Walsh Child Protection Act of 2007 requires that sex offenders as young as fourteen register.

As documented in such reports as Human Rights Watch's "No Easy Answers: Sex Offender Laws in the U.S." and "Registering Harm: How Sex Offense Registries Fail Youth and Communities" from the Justice Policy Institute, conviction and punishment for a sex crime (a term that includes nonviolent offenses such as consensual teen sex, flashing, and patronizing a prostitute) effectively squashes a minor's chances of getting a college scholarship, serving in the military, securing a good job, finding decent housing, and, in many cases, moving forward with hope or happiness.

The sexual dangers to youth, online or off, may be less than we think. Yet adults routinely conflate friendly sex play with hurtful online behavior. "Teaching Teenagers About Harassment," a recent piece in the *New York Times,* swings between descriptions of consensual photo-swapping and incessant, aggressive texting and Facebook or MySpace rumor- and insult-mongering as if these were similarly motivated—and equally harmful. It quotes the San Francisco-based Family Violence Prevention Fund, which calls sending nude photos "whether it is done under pressure or not" an element of "digital dating violence."

Sober scientific data do nothing to calm such anxieties. Reams of comments flowed into the *New York Times* when it reported Dr. Bogle's findings. *The way TV and MUSIC is promoting sex and explicit content daily and almost on every network,* read one typical post, from the aptly named MsKnowledge, *I would have to say this article is completely naive. The streets are talking and there* [sic] *saying*

head as well as I did her face. You may think this doesn't sound like a problem, but it was. I was discovering the "when do you stop?" issue that seems to saturate a great deal of sapphic sex (the male orgasm, while it lacks a certain something in repeatability, at least provides punctuation). As a result, I often found myself in the unenviable position of wishing I could watch TV instead of coming.

And then there was the reciprocation.

There are very few things I don't like to have in my mouth, and cunt tastes like several of the ones I do. Here, however, is the number of things I like to have jammed up against my face: none. Don't put your hand over my mouth. Don't hold my head when you're kissing me. Don't even *think* about gagging me, you pervert. And, most especially, do not ask me to shove my mouth deeply into what seems all too much like your internal organ.

While cocksucking is not on my top ten list of ways to while away the time—well, let's face it, not even on the top one hundred list—a cock is discernibly an appendage and not a giblet, and it is possible to suck cock without getting pubic hair up your nose. I suffer, it seems, from cunniclaustrophobia. My friend went on to practice her new skill on more appreciative ground, and I returned to my quondam heterosexuality.

But once I had cunt on my mind, it stayed there. The phrase "potential space," used to describe the closed-yet-open paradox of the vaginal vault, developed new echoes and resonances. I became fascinated with the rawness of cunt, tender as a partly healed wound, complex and multifoliate, tremulous and nervy. Even the softest epidermis—say, the skin of a penis—began to seem harsh and repudiating. I wanted in.

And, being the kind of girl I am, *in* is what I got. First a finger, then two, then four, then, with a little fussing and adjusting and several great dripping dollops of lubricant, the whole shebang, swallowed like a rabbit into a python. Surrounded. Massaged. Squeezed tight enough to grind dust off my metacarpals. And, oh my god, the steamy slippery volcanic heat, and the sounds she made, and the sounds I made. I was hooked.

The first time I came while fisting somebody, the somebody was a woman with whom I was, at the time, in love. I floated around moonily for a couple of weeks: that's how profound our love was, that I could come just from putting my hand in her. Then, at a sex party, I was fooling around with another woman, a casual acquaintance, not coincidentally the mother of twins, and what I thought was going to be a little hand job turned into her cunt slurping up my arm like spaghetti. And I came. So much for *that* theory.

Now what I think is that cunts are so magical they can transform one body part into another: a hand into a penis, presto—the power of the portal. If I were to paint a picture of a cunt, it wouldn't be a flower or a seashell: it would be a rosy version of the long vaulted emerald hallway down which Dorothy and her friends tiptoed, terrified and avid, confronting the unthinkable in search of the missing part.

Odysseus had to squeeze between Scylla and Charybdis. I wonder if he came when he made it through.

Next I discovered that cunts also have the power to turn the inanimate into the animate, Pinocchio's wet dream. Strap on an inert hunk of silicone and show it a cunt, and it suddenly wakes up, becomes richly innervated, wired into the brain and the spinal cord. There are, of course, logistical challenges—the woman who invents the target-seeking dildo and thus forever eliminates the awkwardness of "Um, it fell out again," will become the century's most deserving millionairess—but

I learned that every dildo harness is a potential Blue Fairy, turning its owner, should she desire it, into a Real Boy. I purchased several.

Of course, men have their own portals, located in roughly the same vicinity, and these have their own charm: puckered instead of slitted, with their complexities hidden inside rather than peeking out coyly, and with the added mud-puddle pleasure of forbidden earthiness. And I suppose that if nobody in the room has a cunt, this is the next best thing, and maybe someday I'll get as attached to assholes as I am to cunts, but so far I'm just not.

I do, however, like men. And since they don't have cunts, we use mine.

Which is how, after several decades of exuberant metasexuality, I have come to a renewed appreciation of penis-vagina intercourse. Now this simple animal pleasure seems like the most arcane of perversions: there he is, pumping and panting and sweating, thinking he's fucking a woman, seeing breasts and a cunt and an unquestionably female megabutt, not knowing that the hand entwined and spasming in his hair used to be a cock and will be one again soon, not realizing that the nightstand full of silicone isn't a toy box but an organ donor.

And here's the thing: at the moment of orgasm it's not clear to me which of us has the cock and which the cunt. *We* are surrounded and engulfed; *we* are penetrated and invaded. We are through the looking glass, in a place where the most gender-specific of acts has blurred gender into meaninglessness. Now *that's* kinky.

That's the power of cunt. Cunt is the primal fissure. It dissembles and assembles; it transports and transforms; it bridges skin and entrail, orifice and protuberance. It does everything, in fact, but define.

Potential space, indeed.

Bite Me! (Or Don't)
Christine Seifert

Abstinence has never been sexier than it is in Stephenie Meyer's young adult four-book *Twilight* series. Fans are super hot for Edward, a century-old vampire in a seventeen-year-old body, who sweeps teenaged Bella, your average human girl, off her feet in a thrilling love story that spans more than two thousand pages. Fans are enthralled by their tale, which begins when Edward becomes intoxicated by Bella's sweet-smelling blood. By the middle of the first book, Edward and Bella are deeply in love and working hard to keep their pants on, a story line that has captured the attention of a devoted group of fans who obsess over the relationship and delight in Edward's superhuman strength to just say no.

The *Twilight* series has created a surprising new subgenre of teen romance: it's abstinence porn, sensational, erotic, and titillating. And in light of all the recent real-world attention on abstinence-only education, it's surprising how successful this new genre is. *Twilight* actually convinces us that self-denial is hot. Fan reaction suggests that in the beginning, Edward and Bella's chaste but sexually charged relationship was steamy precisely because it was unconsummated—kind of like "Cheers," but with fangs. Despite all the hot "virtue," however, we feminist readers have to ask ourselves if abstinence porn is as uplifting as some of its proponents seem to believe.

Given that teens are apparently still having sex—in spite of virginity rings, abstinence pledges, and black-tie "purity balls"—it might seem that remaining pure isn't doing much for the kids these days anyway. Still, the *Twilight* series is so popular it has done the unthinkable: knocked *Harry Potter* off his pedestal as prince of the young adult genre. The series has sold more than fifty million copies, and *Twilight* fan fiction, fan sites, and fan blogs crowd the Internet. Scores of fans have made the trek to real-life Forks, Washington, where the series is set. The first of a trilogy of film adaptations of the books, starring Kristen Stewart and Robert Pattinson, was scheduled to hit theaters in time for Christmas.

Nowhere was readers' multigenerational infatuation with Bella and Edward's steamy romance more evident than in their "engagement" party at a Sandy, Utah, Barnes & Noble store. On the evening of August 1, 2008, before the fourth book was released, guests flocked to the store wearing formal wedding attire to celebrate the happy fictional couple. Preteen girls in princess dresses, "My Heart Belongs to Edward" stickers plastered to their faces, posed for photos. Grandmothers in flowing gowns or homemade "I Love Edward" T-shirts stood in line to play *Twilight* trivia. Clever teen boys in Edward costumes fought off ersatz Bellas.

The air in the store was electric as fans broke into two groups: the much smaller group of Jacob fans (Jacob is Bella's best friend who is hopelessly in love with her, but it's a doomed relationship since Jacob is a werewolf, a lifelong enemy of the vamps) and the group of rabid Edward fans. The questions of the night were: Will Edward and Bella finally do it? If so, will the magic be ruined when the abstinence message is gone? But nobody seemed to be asking an even more important question: has the abstinence message—however unwittingly—undermined feminist sensibilities?

The answers came sooner than expected. After the engagement party, fans rushed home with their copies of *Breaking Dawn*, only to discover that Edward and Bella go all the way in the first few chapters, after they get married, of course. But it seems that in the context of marriage and parenthood (which comes quickly, natch), Edward and now-nineteen-year-old Bella are just like our traditional grandparents. Or the Moral Majority.

Breaking Dawn's Bella is a throwback to a 1950s housewife, except for the fact that Edward has turned her into a vampire. But this act is one of '50s-esque female self-sacrifice: it's precipitated by Bella's need to let her human self die in order to save their half-vampire baby. Their monstrous offspring is frightening, but what's really frightening is Bella and Edward's honeymoon scene. Edward, lost in his own lust, "makes love" so violently to Bella that she wakes up the next morning covered in bruises, the headboard in ruins from Edward's romp. And guess what? Bella likes it. In fact, she loves it. She even tries to hide her bruises so Edward won't feel bad. If the abstinence message in the previous books was ever supposed to be empowering, this scene, presented early in *Breaking Dawn,* undoes everything.

What's worrisome is that fans are livid about the last book not because of the disturbing nature of Bella and Edward's sexual relationship, but because they consummated it in the first place. Shimmerskin, a poster on the message board Twilightmoms.com, summed it up best for a number of defeated fans: "The first three books were alive with sheer romanticism but I never felt it in [*Breaking Dawn*]. The sweep and scope of a grand love affair in [the first three books] was absent. The brilliantly innocent eroticism that took our breath away was also gone." Some fans are so upset at this loss of "innocence" they've created an online petition demanding answers from Meyer and her publisher, Little, Brown. "We were your faithful fans…" the petitioners write. "We are the people that you asked to come along with you on this journey, and we are disappointed."

Perhaps some of this bitter disappointment stems from book four's departure into adult territory, where Bella becomes a traditional—and boring—teenaged mom. The removal of the couple's sexual tension reveals two tepid, unenlightened people. Neither character has much to offer outside the initial high school romance storyline: Bella doesn't have any interesting hobbies, nor is she particularly engaged in the world around her. Her only activity outside her relationship with Edward seems to be cooking dinner for her father. Edward hangs out with his family, but the bulk of his twenty-four hours a day of wakefulness seems to go to either saving Bella from danger or watching her when she sleeps—you know, that age-old savior/stalker duality. Romantic!

As other feminists like Anna N. on Jezebel.com have pointed out, Edward is a controlling dick, a fact that becomes abundantly clear in the leaked pages of Meyer's first draft of *Midnight Sun,* a retelling of *Twilight* from Edward's perspective. In those pages, available on Meyer's website, Edward imagines what it would be like to kill Bella. "I would not kill her cruelly," he thinks to himself. Ever the gentleman, Edward. His icy calculation of how best to kill Bella is horrifying, and it illustrates the disconnect between the two characters.

By extension, readers who interpreted Edward's reluctance to be near Bella in *Twilight* as evidence of his innocent "crush" on her are forced to recognize that even Edward—the dream guy—is not all he's cracked up to be. Digging into Edward's mind reinforces the old stereotype that underneath it all, even the best guys are calculating vampires, figuring out how to act on their masculine urges. Edward holds all the power, while Bella—and female readers—romanticizes the perfect man who doesn't exist. It's no wonder that *Midnight Sun* has not been widely released: it would likely spark even greater fan ire.

Such disappointment suggests something about the desire readers have for abstinence messages; it may also suggest readers' belief that, pre-sex, Edward and Bella were the perfect couple. In reality, the abstinence message—wrapped in the genre of abstinence porn—objectifies Bella in the same ways that "real" porn might. The *Twilight* books conflate Bella losing her virginity with the loss of other things, including her sense of self and her very life. Such a high-stakes treatment of abstinence reinforces the idea that Bella is powerless, an object—a fact that is highlighted when we get to the sex scenes in *Breaking Dawn*.

Of course the paradox is that the more Meyer sexualizes abstinence, the more we want Bella and Edward to actually have sex. This paradox becomes extra-convoluted when we find out, in a moment that for some is titillating, for others creepy, that sex could literally equal death for Bella. In one scene in *Twilight*, Bella asks Edward in a roundabout way if they would ever be able to consummate their relationship. Edward responds, "I don't think that...that...would be possible for us." Bella responds, "Because it would be too hard for you, if I were that...close?" Yes, Edward tells her. But more than that he reminds her that she's "soft" and "so fragile" and "breakable." "I could kill you quite easily, Bella, simply by accident."

And it's not just Bella's life that's at stake—it's her very humanity. The closer she and Edward get, the more tempting it is for him to bite her and turn her into a vampire, and the conflation of his vampiric and carnal urges is obvious. As *Midnight Sun* reveals, Edward's bloodlust is every bit as potent as his romantic love. It doesn't take a Freudian to read Edward's pulsating, insistent vampire lips pressed against Bella's pale, innocent neck as an analogy for, well, something else. From clandestine meetings in Bella's bedroom to time spent in a forest clearing, Edward almost always has his lips on Bella's neck—a dangerous activity, as we learn in *Twilight* that "the perfume of [Bella's] skin" is an unbearably erotic and tempting scent for Edward. When they do kiss, Bella often loses control of herself, which means Edward must be ever-vigilant in controlling "his need." After their first kiss, Bella asks if she should give him some room. "No," he tells her, "it's tolerable." He goes on, "I'm stronger than I thought." Bella responds, "I wish I could say the same. I'm sorry."

Fan fiction reveals fans' tacit understanding of the serious dangers of sex and the excitement of it, illustrating that readers have picked up on Meyer's analogy where the sexual penetration of Bella's human body is akin to the vampiric penetration of Bella's skin. One piece of fan fiction was posted to TheTwilightSaga.com on June 22, 2008, before the release of the fourth book, by a particularly ardent fan (hardy'sgirl). In the story, Edward and Bella have gotten married and are on their honeymoon. Edward begins kissing Bella (on her neck, of course), and then begins removing her jeans. Bella, with a pounding heart, asks herself, "Would I really let him go all the way?" Keep in mind that within this story, Bella and Edward are married; waffling about "doing it" with your husband might point to the age and maturity of the writer, but it also taps into the fear of intimacy that Meyer establishes in the books. The fan writer picks up on that fear as she continues her story: as Edward becomes more sexually aroused, he turns into something Bella doesn't recognize, and she begins to fight him. The fan writes:

> Edward had become a monster. that dangerous vampire he held hidden away from me...and I was the one about to pay for it...he held my arms above my head pinned onto the bed in iron clasps. i was panicking and my breathing was fast. Edward sat up above me...and the look in his eyes weren't ones ive ever seen before...unless he was about to feed.

The rape fantasy is apparent, of course, but even more salient is the fan writer's subconscious understanding of the theme Meyer has been establishing: that sex is dangerous and men must control themselves. It's a matter of life or death, and ultimately men are in charge.

It's clear from both the books and the fan fiction response to them that Edward has taken on the role of protector of Bella's human blood and chastity, both of which, ironically, are always in peril when Edward is nearby. Bella is not in control of her body, as abstinence proponents would argue; she is absolutely dependent on Edward's ability to protect her life, her virginity, and her humanity. She is the object of his virtue, the means of his ability to prove his self-control. In other words, Bella is a secondary player in the drama of Edward's abstinence.

Reader Shimmerskin again astutely notes, "...it's so clever that these books aren't just about sexual abstinence. Edward is fighting two kinds of lust at the same time. Abstaining from human blood has probably been good practice for tamping down his sexual appetites now that he's with Bella...."

It's arguably clever, sure, but it's also a sad commentary on Bella's lack of power. Ultimately, it's a statement of the sexual politics of Meyer's abstinence message: whether you end up doing the nasty or not doesn't ultimately matter. When it comes to a woman's virtue, sex, identity, or her existence itself, it's all in the man's hands. To be the object of desire in abstinence porn is not really so far from being the object of desire in actual porn.

Hot. Digital. Sexual. Underground.
David Black

The man—or perhaps woman—dressed all in black and wearing a disturbingly realistic leather horse's head sits apparently despondent (given the mask, it's hard to tell, but his or her body is slumped) on a bench across from the stage where three bare-breasted women with candles taped to their nipples pose holding...are they dildos? The lighting is dim, and they are obscured by naked and half-naked dancing bodies. Through a doorway in the cavernous club—Passive Arts Studios near LAX in Los Angeles—Larry, a well-known actor, can see a man dressed like Johnny Depp in *Pirates of the Caribbean* using an Indiana Jones bullwhip on a spread-eagled naked woman. When Larry maneuvers through the crowd of perhaps two hundred at the annual DomCon—Domination Convention—Fetish Ball, he glimpses your average six-and-a half-foot-tall transvestite dominatrix, as well as a bent-over young man being sodomized by a woman wielding a butt plug the size of a sawed-off Louisville Slugger.

A guy in his midseventies—clearly the oldest in the group—in full leather regalia, handcuffs at his belt, whip under his arm, rocks his walker toward the unisex bathroom. "Bet he's seen some things in his time," says a woman in a leather thong with studs through her nipples.

"You mean weirder than this?" asks a man in black slacks and a blue blazer. "You have no idea," the woman says, grinning, and sashays away, headed into the labyrinth of rooms in the back of the club. Two of the orgiasts who have joined Larry at the Fetish Ball come out of the bathroom. Betty, a blonde, and Veronica, a brunette, each take one of Larry's arms. Veronica's husband, Reggie, lags behind, scoping out a woman in a catsuit.

"Can you believe," says Betty, "someone in the bathroom line told us we didn't look like we belonged here?"

Both women are dressed for an evening at the Bar Marmont (casual cocktail dresses), though Veronica may pass muster at the Fetish Ball since she is wearing a long, not quite translucent white gown with nothing underneath.

But it isn't really their scene.

"No one's having any orgasms," Veronica says. Larry takes a last look around the club and heads for the door, following Betty, Veronica and Reggie, who consider themselves a sexual trio. Betty comes to L.A. most weekends to play with Veronica and Reggie. In the past few months, Larry has been involved in orgies with both Betty and Veronica, who are part of a vast sexual underground that's different from the erotic underground of the 1970s and 1980s, the era of Plato's Retreat and Sandstone. It's different in great part because of the influence of the Internet, which makes meeting easier and offers a larger pool of potential playmates.

On the way out, Larry, Betty, Veronica and Reggie pass the smorgasbord, which is serving, among other dishes, meatballs in sauce. "If there's a smorgasbord," a friend told Larry, "eat only prewrapped sandwiches—and avoid the mayonnaise."

A few months earlier, just before Christmas, at about 11:30 on a rainy winter Friday night in Los Angeles, Larry, in sweats and a T-shirt, got a phone call from Mercedes, a dancer he had recently met at a music-video shoot.

"What are you doing?" Mercedes asked.

"Nothing," Larry said. He'd just gotten home from a long day of working on a TV show. "You?"

"I'm at the Velvet Margarita," Mercedes said. "Can I come over?"

"Sure," Larry said. Why not?

They had dated a few times. Successfully. "She's very sexual," Larry says about Mercedes. "She's 'All I want to do is fuck you. I don't want to cuddle. I don't want a boyfriend.' She has a boyfriend"—a minor celebrity—"and she's involved in a culture that is very sexually open." Larry grins. "Incredibly sexually open. Completely sexually open."

Mercedes is part of the Los Angeles Lifestyle, or swingers, scene. For her business she travels frequently and widely. She has contacts in the Lifestyle in most major cities. It's like being a member of a lodge, the Masons or the Elks: no matter where you go, all you have to do is signal your insider status and you're at home. If she visits a city where she doesn't know anyone, she can go on the Internet site she prefers, LifestyleLounge.com, and hook up with people who are into her scene: moderately kinky heterosexual and lesbian encounters.

Larry thought a night with Mercedes would be an uncomplicated way to unwind. Uncomplicated?

Larry had no idea what he was in for. "It was pouring rain," Larry says. "One of those five times a year it rains in L.A. A torrential downpour."

Larry lives in the hills, with a lot of cement steps leading up to his front door. He heard *clack clack clack*...the sound of one... two...three sets of high heels approaching his place. Mercedes couldn't get the front door open. "Larry," Mercedes explains, "is an obsessive door locker."

The worst rainstorm of the year. Mercedes pounded on the door. When Larry finally opened it, he saw Mercedes drenched, her blonde hair wet and pasted to her forehead and cheeks, in a black trench coat. With another beautiful woman, Betty, also drenched, in a black trench coat and high heels. And a beautiful Asian woman, Kathy, also drenched, in a black trench coat and high heels. Their hair, before it was soaked, had been done up so they all looked like librarians. Larry said, "Hi, hi, hi. Whatever is going on here?"

The three women came into his foyer, each pulling a rolling suitcase containing whatever she thought might come in handy during the night. "Everyone came with her own toys," Larry explains. "Vibrators, dildos, this little vibrating handy thing. I don't know what it was. It looks like a computer mouse." The Mouse, the Butterfly, the Rabbit, the Penguin—vibrators come with names that make them seem as innocuous as Disney cartoon characters.

Larry offered to take their coats.

"He was trying to be a gentleman," Mercedes explains.

She, Betty and Kathy got the giggles. They knew what the coats covered: underneath they were wearing nothing but lingerie. Larry says, "I was like, Why, I never! I do declare!"

But, Larry says, "I knew exactly what was going to happen." He grins. "Dreams do come true."

"Larry didn't miss a beat," Mercedes recalls.

His face registered no shock. No surprise. "What did Bear Bryant say about scoring a touchdown?" Larry says. "Act like you've been there before."

Mercedes and her friends looked, Mercedes says, "like drowned rats. It wasn't sexy at all."

Larry disagrees.

At dinner, before Mercedes called Larry, she had suggested to her two girlfriends that they surprise him with a spontaneous foursome. She told Betty and Kathy, "Let's ruin his life. We're going to ruin his life because once someone has a taste for this it's hard to go back."

"We thought we were going to ruin him for straight girls," Betty says, "which didn't turn out to be the case." Like many women in the Lifestyle, Betty refers to women as girls. "We were disappointed," she says. "We wanted a little more shock and helplessness," as though Larry had no idea this kind of thing—threesomes, foursomes, orgies—existed. "Instead," Betty says, "he took the reins."

Typically, Mercedes says, you put a guy who is not part of the Lifestyle scene "in that situation and he's going to go for his comfort zone. He's going to go for me," the woman he knows. But Larry didn't. "He grabbed my girlfriend Betty," Mercedes says, "threw her on the couch and started eating her out. Kathy and I looked at each other. The party was on!"

Mercedes told Larry, "No fingers."

"What do you mean?" Larry asked.

"No fingers," Mercedes repeated. "What did I say? No fingers."

Those were the rules Mercedes laid down. "You can suck only," she explained.

Betty started laughing.

"We tell people what we want them to do," Mercedes says, "so you don't have to do the fishing expedition."

"Next thing you knew," Larry recalls, "I had Kathy sucking my cock. Mercedes was underneath me, licking my balls. I was like, fantastic! I'd never had a threesome or foursome before."

It was, Larry decided, geometrically better: each added person multiplied possibilities. "There's so much stimulus," Larry explains, "everything gets sensitized." It became hard to focus on any particular body part—his or his partners'. "You just join the aroma around you," Larry says. As in a square dance, they changed partners—and positions. Although Kathy told Larry, "I'm sorry I can't let you fuck me in the ass. I broke my tailbone the other day playing roller hockey."

"Kathy's great to play with," Mercedes says. "Easy to play with. Never gets upset about anything."

There was a lot of bending, but no breaking, of rules. "Three rounds," Mercedes says. "Amazing fun. I set it up purely for me, the most selfish moment in my life."

"You should be selfish more often," Larry laughs.

That rainy night Larry also didn't leave anyone out. "Whoever I was with at the time," Larry says, "it was like she was the only one there, not like I was looking over her shoulder at who was next." He shrugs. "I only have one cock!"

Mercedes thought Larry was special not just because he took control but because he didn't assume this was his birthright. A guy who isn't wired right will expect an orgy "every time he sees you, rather than understand this isn't easy to pull off."

Still, the instantaneous and ubiquitous communication

available because of the Internet and texting makes it easier than ever to pull off, as Larry would soon learn. After the women left, at 4:30 in the morning, Larry sat gazing into space, thinking, *I have a very good life...*

Since the arrival of the Internet, the swingers scene Mercedes, Betty, Kathy, Veronica and Reggie—and now Larry—are part of has exploded both numerically and geographically. In the past, people interested in alternative sex had to find partners through ads in the back of specialty magazines like *Connections, Spectator* and *Select,* which were hard to find in some areas. They had to send letters and wait for responses. After a number of exchanges, when everyone felt safe and comfortable, people might make phone calls to get a sense of the others from the sound of their voice and the immediacy of the interchange. After enough phone calls, people might meet in bars or, if they lived in large enough cities, seek out swingers clubs. All that effort was shaded by a sense of potential ostracism.

Now, with the Internet, Craigslist, MySpace, Yahoo or any of the many adult-oriented sites like LifestyleLounge.com, Alt.com, Blissparty.com, AdultPartyQuest.com, Fling.com, Swappernet.com, PrivateSoiree.com, SwingLifeStyle.com and AdultFriendFinder.com (which Peter Cook visited, according to his ex-wife Christie Brinkley), people can instantly be put in contact with hundreds, even thousands of potential swing partners, for either hard swinging (parties where it is assumed couples will trade partners) or soft swinging (parties where swapping is available but not assumed).

One typical site—SwingersClubList.com—advertises itself as "the most up-to-date free worldwide directory for the swinging lifestyle, with listings in the following categories: swingers clubs, parties/groups, hotels/B&Bs, shops, online business and literature, easily sorted by name, location, reviews and ratings." Its "Favorite Swinging Places Rated by Swingers" includes "personals, parties, gangbangs...." "For those who want more than just one bite of the apple"—presumably the apple Eve offered to Adam—the North American Swing Club Association International, or NASCA, offers information about "on/off premises clubs, travel and resorts, publication listings, conventions and events, Internet services...breaking news, frequently asked questions...and swing club franchise opportunities." This is no back-alley sneak-around community.

The Internet has turned swinging into a multimillion-dollar industry that is growing every year, involving—according to Dr. Robert McGinley, founder of NASCA—at least four hundred clubs in the United States with perhaps three million American participants. AdultFriendFinder.com claims to have 31,959,644 members. Even smaller and less metropolitan states boast sizable subscriber numbers, like Alabama, which allegedly has 226,661, and Utah, which allegedly has 135,219.

Alt.com claims to be the "world's largest BDSM and alternative lifestyle personals" site. It has, according to its own accounting, 2,932,224 members—again, not just in large cities. Even Guam has a membership of 716. American Samoa has 34. The Lifestyle scene changes from city to city. "It's very geographical," Veronica explains on the way to the Fetish Ball. "Some cities don't have a scene." Other cities have scenes that are specific to the particular erotic DNA of the local culture. Los Angeles, not surprisingly, tends to be into exhibitionism and voyeurism. New York, the financial capital of the country, tends to be more into S/M, BD and DS: power. Reggie dismisses New York. "Not happening," he says. "From the neck down, nothing happening." Too intellectual—although that may betray his Los Angeles bias. Maybe in the suburbs. Westchester County. Connecticut. New Jersey.

San Francisco is "more artsy," Veronica says. "Unusual. Eclectic."

"Miami is very into drugs," Reggie says. "Late nights. Ecstasy."

Dallas?

"Very stratified," Reggie says.

"Denver has a good scene," Veronica says.

"Denver," Betty agrees, "is a free-spirited, open-minded city."

They circle back to New York and agree that Giuliani destroyed the scene.

From the moment Larry and Mercedes spotted each other on a music-video set—Larry was visiting a friend, Mercedes was training dancers—it was lust at first sight. If this had been one of Larry's movies, everyone else would have faded into the background. The soundtrack would have become muffled, and they would have moved toward each other in slow motion as the camera made a 360-degree pan. Their relationship also developed quickly because Mercedes was ready for an adventure. "Three weeks earlier," Mercedes says, "I'd been at a business meeting with a guy and his partner, who was ridiculously good-looking." They were at the bar at the Standard, on Sunset Strip. The man Mercedes had met for business had an early call the next morning. "You guys keep talking," he said—and left.

"I knew I wasn't going to have any dealings with this guy again," Mercedes explains, so she set out to bed the good-looking partner.

"So," Mercedes asked, "you live around here?"

"As a matter of fact," the partner said, "I live in a loft right down the street."

Mercedes thought, *Hmmm*... "Are you married?" she asked him.

"No."

"Do you have a live-in girlfriend?"

"No."

"Do you want to go back to your place?" Mercedes asked.

"What?"

"I have a hall pass from my boyfriend," Mercedes explained. "He says I'm welcome to go home with you if I want to. And I want to."

"Shouldn't we do the responsible thing and get to know each other first?"

"Absolutely not," Mercedes said. "I don't want to know you."

He ordered another drink. Mercedes said, "Check, please."

This became a running joke between Mercedes and her boyfriend: I give you a hall pass, and you can't close the deal! So when Mercedes met Larry, she thought, *I'm going to get this one done!* She was intrigued. She liked Larry. He didn't seem needy. He was laid-back. Honest. Which, Mercedes says, is "very, very rare among single men. He never told me what he thought I wanted to hear. He never looked like he had an agenda."

"So," Mercedes asked Larry, "what do you do?"

"I'm an actor," Larry said.

"You make a living as an actor?" Mercedes asked.

"Yeah," he said.

"I was a bitch," Mercedes later says.

She gave him a hard time, but she didn't much care who or what he was. They went out three times before she thought to Google him and discovered, "Oh, he's for real." He was a suc-

cessful actor. As Mercedes left the shoot, she was already texting Larry: HOW SOON CAN WE GET TOGETHER?
WHAT ARE YOUR FANTASIES? she texted.
WHAT ARE YOUR FANTASIES? he texted.
"I'd tell him a story," Mercedes says. "He'd add on. Then I'd add on. Then he would." Through texting and email Mercedes almost instantly discovered Larry "liked the side of sex I liked." Master-slave role-playing.

"I think people feel more free texting," Mercedes says. "I definitely talk more freely in text. I don't do phone sex so well. I change the subject."

"When we first met," Larry says, "I was out of town a lot. Texting kept the interest growing. We had a bet to see who could make the other masturbate first using email and text. So when we got together it was explosive."

Texts flashed back and forth between them.

"We pushed the pedal to the metal," Mercedes says, "and were going two hundred miles an hour. We knew where the other was fantasy-wise before we even got together." Technology lubricated their relationship. What might have taken a month or two to develop twenty years earlier—maybe during a dozen dinners and two dozen late-night conversations as they edged deeper into their erotic jungle—happened almost instantly.

"Watch people texting," one orgiast says. "The constant tapping of keys, the rapt expression—it even looks like someone masturbating."

Unlike Larry—who sees himself as a sexual tourist—Mercedes is a sexual hobbyist. Larry indulges occasionally; for Mercedes, the Lifestyle is a lifestyle.

She stumbled onto the scene fifteen years ago, when she was

twenty-one. She used to go to a resort in Loreto, Mexico, called Diamond Eden, between Cabo and La Paz. She didn't notice anything unusual about the place until she and her girlfriend went one Halloween.

"Even on the plane it was kind of odd," Mercedes says. "Ninety percent of the people were also going to the resort. A guy was walking around the plane with a clipboard, checking people off."

He asked Mercedes and her friend their names and scanned the list. Nope, they weren't on the roster. He walked away. At the resort, they were sitting by the pool when Clipboard Guy came up to them and said, "You weren't on my list."

"What list?" Mercedes asked.

Clipboard Guy thought they were part of an organization that was meeting there, Lifestyles.

What's Lifestyles? Mercedes wondered.

She began to pay more attention.

There were, she noticed, a lot of people wandering around naked, being unusually affectionate.

"I ended up dating a guy who was part of the organization," Mercedes says. "A bodybuilder."

She still has friends she met on that weekend fifteen years ago.

"There's no division," Mercedes explains, "between my life and the Life."

But that doesn't mean she isn't discreet, she says. She was in a restaurant with a dozen friends from the Lifestyle scene, and one couple was being obvious about their swinger association. Across the room was "a client of mine," Mercedes explains. She started distancing herself from the obstreperous couple, but the woman in the couple said, at the top of her lungs, "I don't give a shit who knows I'm a swinger."

"Needless to say," Mercedes adds, "I got a call the next day from my client, who said, 'I don't want to be affiliated with that.' I lost a one-thousand-two-hundred-dollar-a-month client."

The foursome in the rain was so successful Mercedes decided she wanted Larry to host a pussy party: Larry, Mercedes, Betty, Kathy—and four of Mercedes's friends who are part of the scene, including Veronica, who came without Reggie on the condition that she could play with the other women but not with Larry. Seven women and one man.

Since the foursome, Larry had played with Mercedes and Betty, but none of them considered that an orgy: three people doesn't rise to their definition of what constitutes an orgy. If four is the lower limit of an orgy, what is the upper?

Larry and Mercedes exchange glances. With more than a dozen, they agree, it becomes hard to keep track of people—although theoretically there is no upper limit.

When she throws parties at her house, "I limit it to twenty or thirty couples," Mercedes says. "And I have a wait list." But she prefers smaller parties.

"Two on two," she says, "three on three…"

Even with such a low number there's "so much pressure," Mercedes says. "Four people have to like one another. Hard to get that dynamic to work." Think of it as dating: Even one-on-one it can be hard to find the right match. What about parties with other men?

"If I had fifty women," Larry admits, "I wouldn't mind another guy—across the room."

Mercedes wanted to throw the pussy party at Larry's primarily to give each woman a chance to act out a favorite fantasy "no matter what it was," she says. "I wanted to do something just for the girls." One wanted to hang out with her girlfriends. Another wanted to watch. Another, according to Mercedes, "just wanted strange." Betty had "an intimate connection" with Larry, whom she considered her "imaginary boyfriend." Mercedes wanted Larry to read aloud from her favorite book, the first volume of Anne Rice's erotic trilogy *The Claiming of Sleeping Beauty*. She told Larry, "This is who I am." But Mercedes may also have been trying to draw Larry back in.

Larry had been so busy with business—acting gigs, trips to New York—that Mercedes felt he was neglecting her. One of her many text messages read, I CAN'T BELIEVE YOU'RE NOT HERE. I'M IN BED AT THE STANDARD WITH A DILDO UP MY ASS. WISH IT WAS YOUR COCK, BUT YOU'RE NOT HERE. YOU MADE YOUR CHOICE.

Remember the old telephone ad, "Reach out and touch someone"? With the Internet, that's more possible than ever before.

A pussy party might get Larry's attention. The only rule Mercedes gave Larry was no touching. He was there as a butler. A majordomo. A boy Friday. Serving only. Larry grew up in a household with his divorced mother and three sisters, two older, one younger, whom he raised. He explains, "Giving a woman a nice time when they don't have to do shit pleases me."

"His role for the night was supposed to be like a page—to get things," Mercedes explains. "It was never supposed to progress to where it did."

They timed it so that when the women arrived Larry had a bubble bath waiting, candles lit, wine poured, beer on ice. "It couldn't have been a more diverse group of women," Larry says. It was like having a harem made up of the Seven Dwarfs. Very sexy, lithe and lovely dwarfs: Sexy, Sleepy, Sleazy, Bashful…

Larry got them drinks. A kiss here. A kiss there. Then he was in his underpants, leaning back against the headboard of his bed, with the women stretched out around him on the mattress. One of them cuddled up to his left, wearing white panties with pink stripes around the leg holes and a white shirt with a pink oval pattern. Another woman was to his right. A naked woman leaned faceup against his chest while Mercedes—wearing red-and-pink striped panties, a white short-sleeved shirt and a small-brimmed hat—lay facedown between her open legs.

"Within ten minutes," Larry says, one of the women, Dawn, "had my cock in her hand."

Things got rolling—or, as Mercedes thought, out of control. "I'd be fucking one," Larry says. "Some would be watching. Some going down on me. Some going down on each other."

Three of the women ran to the bathroom and started making out in the bubble bath. More wine flowed.

"The problem is the reality of these things," Veronica says. "There's always some catastrophe."

One of the three girls got out of the tub and grabbed a towel. Which was caught under a painting. Which fell. In the bedroom, when Larry heard the glass shattering, he thought, *Great, the best night of my life, and I'm going to end up in the emergency room!*

In the bathroom "everyone froze," Veronica says. "Three girls in the bath with broken glass and wine and…." Larry ran in. Everyone was all right. But the bathroom—and the rest of the house—was a wreck. Larry started to clean up, but Mercedes said, "Get out of here. We'll take care of it."

The women went into action, picking up the glass and putting salt and seltzer water on the wine-stained sheets. After they finished cleaning up, Mercedes corralled the others and told them,

"You girls are going to fuck the shit out of him because you're fucking up his place."

The story of the Seven Women Who Destroyed a Guy's House has become legendary in the Los Angeles Lifestyle scene. For the rest of the night, until 6:30 the next morning, Larry remembers, "every orifice, every part of my body was being touched by a tongue, a pussy. I was fucking this girl. There was this girl going down on another girl. There were tits all over." If this had been a movie, Larry thinks, the daisy chain would have made a great dolly shot. One of the women prided herself on giving the best blow jobs in L.A. Larry says, "She was going to town. Mercedes and Betty were watching, and they were like, 'If you blow your load, we're going to fucking kill you.' And I didn't. They loved that."

Was it the best blow job in L.A.? It was, Larry admitted, maybe a nine-point-three.

Larry spent a good part of the night doing multiplication tables to "keep from putting myself out of business."

At one point all seven women were on their backs as Larry went from one to the other to the next. Licking. Like a vaudeville performer keeping seven plates spinning on seven poles. One, Larry says, tasted like a bold merlot, another like a light white wine, another like springwater...

Unlike the swingers scene thirty or forty years ago, which was driven by men, the scene today is driven by women—which made the pussy party at Larry's not at all unusual—at least not within the Lifestyle. Mercedes supplied the soundtrack for the party. "Women are responsible for their own orgasms and the soundtrack," Larry says. "That's going to be my platform when I run for president."

★ ★ ★

At their orgies, Veronica and Reggie like to play naked Jingo. "Or the name game," she says. "All sorts of stupid games. We watch one another have fun and be silly and hang out and then go and have sex. It's all sort of seamless."

People in the Lifestyle scene autosort: "Couples find their own niche," Veronica says. "Just like in high school."

The people into kink hang together. The people into sexy outfits hang together. The people into drugs hang together, though there aren't as many drugs as one may suppose. "Mostly ecstasy," Mercedes says, "and Viagra and Cialis…."

Harder drugs like coke or even softer drugs like pot make people dysfunctional—both sexually and socially. "And it's more fun if you can have a conversation," Veronica says.

During the Night of the Seven Women, Larry recalls, "You'd think the conversation would have been very light. But I had deeper conversations than I would on my third or fourth date with somebody normal," outside the scene. "Everything from child rearing to psychology. Most of the time when a guy asks a girl about where she grew up, et cetera, it's about getting laid. I'm already getting laid, so if I ask a girl anything or if she asks me, it's real. I realized an hour in, when they asked a simple question like 'How many sisters do you have?' they really wanted to know. There's no bullshit." The women at the orgy confirmed that Larry's charm and authenticity made the evening work. Most guys available online are the same type: Arizona, buffed, chinos, short streaky blond hair, a little too tan, shirt a little too tight. Two generations ago it would have been George Hamilton. Just a tool.

Some people seek anonymity in their orgies: anonymous bodies to rub against. In fact, for some the anonymity is what counts. But more often than not people in the scene describe that phenomenon as old-school, the way people approached orgies in the past. Today the orgiasts seem to be searching for the same thing the characters on "Friends" and "Seinfeld" search for: when we leave home and move to the big city, who will be our family?

"The pure sex," Larry says, "only lasts for so long."

Even for those just looking for a "tool," it seems to be as hard to find a good date in the Lifestyle community as it is in the vanilla community and for some of the same reasons, especially the proportion of appropriate available males to available females. Over and over, women in the scene complain there aren't that many men out there. Unless you get to know the other person as a person and have a relationship, Veronica thinks, it's just friction.

"It's a lot more comfortable when you know the people," Betty agrees. "You're a lot more free to relax and enjoy it, to express yourself. Especially for a single woman."

"The more people involved," Mercedes says, "the more inappropriate people are involved."

Which is the downside of the Internet. It has made hooking up too easy. And oddly, orgiasts do not like that kind of promiscuity, which encourages people who don't get the rules to join in.

"Eleven, twelve years ago, everyone just flocked together," Mercedes explains. You'd go to a Lifestyle resort and see "a celebrity sitting next to a plumber in his fifties." It was more democratic. But there's a difference between erotic democracy and the erotic mob. Increasingly, "no didn't mean no anymore," Mercedes says. Men became more aggressive, expecting—demanding—sex from any woman at a party, whether or not the woman wanted to play. Mercedes noticed the change six years ago at a Halloween party.

"Some guy just walked up behind me," she says, "and I was like, I don't know who the hell you are."

Rejected, the guy threatened Mercedes, who had to go to the party master and have the man ejected.

At big parties, "people don't screen anymore," Mercedes says. "Safety has gone out the door, and you have to feel safe to feel sexy." The big-party scene also became more and more commercial.

"I resent paying two hundred dollars to go to a party that doesn't have good music and you have to bring your own alcohol," Mercedes says. For a lot less, she says, "I can get a group of my friends together and rent a house for the weekend."

Or use Larry's house…

Betty, Veronica and Reggie have also moved away from the big-party scene. That scene—like the weekly Bliss parties in Los Angeles—is about sex and profits. Their orgies are about sex and love. The three of them have been intimate for four years. Some marriages among their friends haven't lasted that long. Most weekends, Betty comes into Los Angeles and stays and plays with Veronica and Reggie, who drop their kids off at their grandparents' house. They have had Thanksgivings and birthdays together and met each other's families.

"I had no idea it was going to get as deep or intense as it got as fast as it got," Veronica says. Taking Reggie's arm protectively, she adds, Betty's "our girlfriend." How does that work? Does it work? Clearly, among the three of them, they are not—monogamous? Triogamous? "No, no," Reggie says, "there's always room for pretty women."

Pretty women. Unmentioned are handsome men. But the women—like the men—like women. The scene is a gynarchy, in which men like women who like women. "When we started being with Betty regularly," Veronica says, "all of a sudden everything changed. The sex was exponentially better because of the emotional connection. We knew who she was, knew what made her..."

"With someone you don't know," Betty says, "there are always concerns, issues."

"She's seen us in our darkest hours," Veronica says.

"And you've seen me in mine," Betty says, turning to Veronica and Reggie. "It just seems so natural." Jealousy?

"Communication," Reggie says.

"From my perspective," Betty adds, "this is the most perfect relationship in the world. How could there be any jealousy? I'm in the easiest position, having nothing to lose."

But the best part, all three agree, is not the sex; it's the cuddling after sex. The spooning. Adds Veronica, "And the pancakes the next morning."

Betty, Veronica and Reggie plan to buy a house together in Northern California and live together with Veronica's and Reggie's kids from their previous marriages. Will it work?

Larry's priorities are different. "I'm not so committed to the scene," he says. He sees his foray into the Life ending in three different ways. "First," he says, "in a Garry Marshall kind of way: Mercedes brings someone, we hit it off, she's Ms. Right, and we walk off into the sunset. Second, I meet Ms. Right, but Mercedes freaks out and grabs a carving knife—the *Basic Instinct* ending. Third, the *Big Love* ending: 'Honey, I'm home. Honey and Honey and Honey.'"

On the night following the Domination Convention's Fetish Ball, Larry, Betty, Veronica and Reggie jump into a limo and cruise through the Los Angeles night. They discuss what to do with the rest of the evening. Drop by the weekly Bliss party to hang with the couple hundred gawkers and stalkers? Drinks at the Sunset Marquis? Back to the Chateau Marmont, where they had started the night having dinner three tables over from Drew Barrymore, two tables over from Robert Downey Jr. and across from one of the Olsen twins?

"What I want," Veronica says, dismissing the fetishists at the ball, "is to go home and have some good old-fashioned hot sex."

Loving Lesbians
William Georgiades

A large woman with a teenage scruff of beard on her chin was swallowing fire as the band played. The lead singer, not to be outdone in getting attention, stripped to the waist to reveal a chain leading from one clamped nipple to the other. Protruding from her pelvis was a large, black strap-on dildo, which had been a great deal bigger before being cut in half to cheers from the audience. Forty or so women (and less than a handful of men) swayed to the thrashing sounds emanating from the foursome backing up this fearsome creature as she screeched out the lyrics: "Neanderthal dyke, Neanderthal dyke, feminist theory gets me uptight." I had arrived.

If to kiss and tell is considered less gentlemanly than to not kiss, to merely pine, then telling must be deemed less than manly. Or more poetic, along the lines of sorrowful Young Werther. I spent most of my twenties, that period that might be sleekly compartmentalized as the majority of my sex life, in the otherwise sleepy college town of Northampton, Massachusetts, a town that had the distinction of being dubbed the lesbian capital of America. The title had been bestowed by two different news mediums, the resolutely down-market weekly magazine, *The National Enquirer,* and the slightly more respected television show, "20/20."

In both stories women were shown to be cavorting down Main Street hand in hand, making out with wild abandon and, somewhat less excitingly, discussing the sociopolitical ramifications inherent in their sapphic Eden. Men were given short shrift. For the purpose of news we were either angry or docile, the latter example shown wearing a pin with the words: *I'm a lesbian trapped inside a man's body.*

At the time of all this media commotion, I worked in a coffee shop and was blissfully unaware of the estrogen-charged atmosphere. To the right of the coffee shop was a radical feminist bookshop (their words) and to the left a lingerie store. Between the two I washed dishes while listening to my Walkman, ignoring the lesbian folksingers who invariably occupied the stage. My indoctrination into the fresh obsession of bedding lesbians, or more to the point, attempting to bed lesbians, occurred in that strictly appropriate context of menial labor betwixt feminist tomes and fancy pants.

A coworker as unfriendly as myself explained with grave matter-of-factness that she was a lesbian who had never been with a man of her own volition. Further (and this was shared over a conspiratorial cigarette by the Dumpster in the alley), she had recently come under the sway of a rather militant group of women whose very earnestness, not to mention hate, made her want to rebel out of sheer cussedness. If, she reasoned quite reasonably, she was to stay true to the cause for the rest of her life, then she wanted to know what she was missing. It was not the warmest of romantic approaches, but that only made me the more enthusiastic. The implicit suggestion was that for my colleague sex with a man was the ultimate taboo, the kink to beat all kinks, a mindfuck more potent than any physical act, something to challenge and perplex her reading list, rallies, convictions and beliefs. Talk about performance anxiety! But I reflected that though I would be judged solely as I compared to the fairer sex, I also barely figured in her equation at all. I just happened to be washing dishes in the right place at the right time.

What struck me most in that heretofore gay bedroom with its posters of Jodie Foster was that for all intents and purposes I was with a virgin, a sensual and accomplished virgin, well-trained, as it were, but fresh to combat. It was the first time I'd been with someone technically chaste; that she happened to be an able partner only added to the thrill. My technical usefulness did not last long—friendships based on decontextualizing social parameters tend not to be the firmest of foundations—and this young woman exited my life as brutally as I suppose I had entered hers.

That first encounter, hot and heavy though it may have been, was a tease, a drug dealer's first free taste of his (or her) narcotic, after which one has to pay for one's pleasure. The taste had been acquired. The metaphor is apt, and I hasten to add that this was a taste, not a sport. I did not fancy myself as so irresistible that straight girls became too easy for me. Neither did lesbians present themselves as some worthy challenge. I was not so vigorously heterosexual that I felt the need to personally welcome each and every gay woman I came across back to more traditional frontiers. As with any addiction (and I write in a culture in which anything pleasant is deemed an addiction), there was no plan for the course things would take. I merely became aware of an itch that had to be scratched.

For my dishwashing colleague, sleeping with me had been a way of pushing the boundaries to their farthest extreme. For myself, the scenario appealed to my inherent conservatism. Concepts such as courtship, wooing and flirting entered my life for the first time, the notion of a delicacy of exchange between the sexes being utterly new to me. Most of the gay girl flings I had subsequently were, by their very nature, a shade too chaste for my hormonal wishes, but it was that very factor of the sex act being an impossibility that I found most enticing. One loves what one cannot have more fiercely than anything, especially at that age. And so, in my own way, I constructed a reality close to my perception of a bygone era where clothes were never shed and a glimpse of bare ankle was considered risqué (never minding that skin was on constant display).

My love of lesbians had little to do with an appreciation for any cause or belief and everything to do with objectification. Here were women who could be romanticized and idealized out of all human recognition. They were the princesses that boys with horses might dream of finding, untouchable and therefore perfect.

Flush and smug with success I began to make friends with the impenetrable crew of trendy downtown dykes who frequented the coffee house I worked in. Cambria was the first to allow me into her life, a hardy woman far tougher and more manly than I ever wanted to be. We whiled away one summer at sidewalk cafes comparing women and engaging in such sordid physical exertions as tennis, softball, kayaking and hiking, all of which she excelled at far more than me. I was endlessly inquisitive, fascinated by her existence, her friends, everything. She told me once that the problem with being gay, even in a community such as ours, was that once she had established attraction it was always difficult to know if the object of her affection shared her bent, let alone the affection. The dilemma was made more acute by the fact that she was taken with feminine women. It was in the course of this conversation that I began to gather a rudimentary, working vocabulary, an emotional fluency.

There were two distinct camps, butch and femme. While my male contemporaries were judging women's hair color and bust size, I was getting hung up on gender bias within one gender. I would see a girl I liked the look of and be told she was too girly-girl, too fluffy to be a proper femme (the same problem Cambria tended to have). The distinction became ever more subtle; college girls were especially suspect serving as they were their four-year terms with a trendy alternative lifestyle only to become that most dreaded of creatures, what I myself was, a breeder. A traditional lesbian relationship was distressingly familiar. There would be the butch or daddy dyke and the femme or lipstick lesbian. Then there were the leather dykes, a supposedly hardcore faction of the butch set, given to edge play such as piercing, branding and old fashioned S/M. I recall seeing some of these women at play once and having the immediate, unkind thought that they were like little girls playing at Cowboys and Indians and getting it all disastrously wrong.

There were other terms: women were *wimmin* or *womyn*. Girls as such had ceased to exist (unless they went to the local colleges) and in their place had risen *grrrls*. Instead of a girlfriend one's beloved was referred to as *partner*. And then there were the two terms that defined me: *het* and *beard*. A beard, it transpired, was just a fuzzy name for that old traditional standby, the walker, socially acceptable and unthreatening.

My agenda, odd though it may have been, was clear, at least to me. Quite why I was considered socially acceptable by these womyn was more mysterious though. We did have much in common: alienation, unfocused rage, various aesthetics. But there was something more binding, more definitive of our characters, stretching back to childhood. Helplessness, powerlessness produces the most profound rage. Phrases such as "There are no victims, only willing participants" had a particular resonance in our group. Further, the lightest of lives tend to be built on the heaviest of pasts, roses from manure, if you will. What we all had in common was gaiety, hard-won, in the old fashioned sense of the word.

All went well for a dizzying time, the only obvious problem being that once I was in a relationship with a lesbian she wasn't really a lesbian anymore and my interest would soon wane. Despite Gore Vidal's maxim that there are no homosexuals or heterosexuals, only homosexual and heterosexual acts, I soon found that the only people who were making sense to me were the diehard gay grrrls. One after another my sexual relationships (mostly with these same college girls) would tumble into the horrifying regularity of het dullness and I would spend most of my time with my newfound set, much to the relevant girlfriend's annoyance. She had, after all, left that group, or one like it, for me (often to considerable disparagement) while I remained a part of it.

This was masculine callousness, to be sure, to meet womyn within a group of lesbians, woo them and have them turn into women, into girlfriends, and then leave them, bit by bit, by sticking with the grrrls. The women I was attracted to, the women who were my friends, held that penetrative sex was completely beyond the pale and so they found it hard to relate or identify with anyone who would willingly be penetrated or, god forbid, perform fellatio. Penetration was a violation, clitoral orgasms would suffice (separating them from the dildo-wielding leather daddy dykes). They were the nonpenetrative majority and in the same swift certain way they had entered my life socially and emotionally, so too did I begin to get steeped in the culture involved.

There were the bands that provided the soundtrack for those days: Scrawl, Lunachicks, 7 Year Bitch and Babes in Toyland, all as angry, churning and unmelodic as myself. I attended comedy revues wherein the comedienne's entire act was built on her sexual identity. Lea Delaria is the only name I recall of that ilk. She was, it was whispered, about to become famous and indeed, for a time, her face would appear on television. This was the early to mid-1990s when lesbianism per se was making its biggest cultural foray. Radio shock jock Howard Stern noted loudly and often that the very word *lesbian* was a boon to ratings. Movie stars and singers were variously outed and the sin of pride became the watchword for alternate togetherness. (The symbol was a pink triangle, an image that graced every second or third car that would drive by.) None of this was new, of course—lovely Sappho had gotten the ballslessness rolling a couple millennium beforehand—but there was a zeitgeist in effect and I was squarely in the right place at the right time.

There were Take Back the Night Marches, complete with candlelit vigils for those taken in the night. There was an annual lesbian festival that drew thousands from across the country. There were art exhibits of hardcore lesbian erotica and one artist in particular, Yohah Ralph, looked set to make a huge splash on the scene. There were magazines—*Bad Attitude, Off Our Backs* (and the cheeky *On Our Backs*), *Bikini Kill* and *Yellow Silk,* all as happily pornographic as they were vitriolic, all of which I happened to come across as the required reading list for a university course on gender. And then there were the speakers, the "sex positives" who did the lecture circuit. I met Lydia Lunch, Susie Bright and Annie Sprinkle, the highlight of whose show consisted of a personal viewing of her cervix with aid of a speculum. One happy day there was what I came to think of as the sex-negative speaker, Andrea Dworkin, who was as fiery as she was contradictory. She was anti-men and married. She was antipornography but had written a pornographic book called *Fire and Ice,* intended, she said, for women only. "A woman on the street for twenty-four hours is safer than a woman alone at home with a man," she roared to riotous applause in a packed Smith College auditorium.

And so to the bearded, fire-eating lady and the topless, nipple-clamped singer. The band was called Tribe 8, the verb "to tribate" apparently having something to do with the rubbing of female genitalia on their partner's leg. Their singer, a Ms. Lynn Breedlove, provided my favorite songs, "Fem Bitch Top" and "Neanderthal Dyke." She also endeared herself by railing against the likes of Ms. Dworkin. Feminist theory made us both uptight, but she had a particular eloquence, not to mention credibility, that I lacked. "Fuck you middle-aged white woman who tells me how to fuck," she roared. That moment in the club relaxed me utterly. Though it would bring Ms. Breedlove no comfort to know it, she let me know that I did fit in even as she took a knife to her already mutilated dildo.

Defining moments have a way of destroying conviction, the certainty one fit into a world where nobody fit and, more to the point, fit into a world I could never really fit in. I started to lose the thread. In the topsy-turvy scheme of things, I had finally thrown caution to the wind and fallen for a straight girl. She had promptly moved to San Francisco, the gay men's capital of

America. At the time I was hanging out almost constantly with three womyn: Angie, Vicky and Kate, all three gently swaying from butch to femme as the feeling moved them, and all three very approving of my newfound love. (Lesbians, after all, have some interest in turning het girls.) Angie was an eminently adorable young womyn, who had moved from California for no discernible reason with her girlfriend. We had become the best of friends, with the help of our dogs (mine female, hers male) and a shared passion for running. Every morning Angie would come to my house, wake me and take me out running before I'd gained consciousness. On a whim, she agreed to drive to San Francisco with me, clear across the country. The Great Het Adventure, she called it.

She told me at the outset that I was exhibiting all the male traits that reminded her of why she'd never wanted to be with a man—machismo, pride and some obscure sense of ownership (my plan was to bring my girlfriend back to Northampton). Oddly, this didn't keep her from liking me enough to join me. En route we were sleeping together, as we did from time to time, in the manner that perhaps brothers and sisters might. She woke me, as was her wont, with a chaste kiss. I was still somewhat involved in an unchaste dream concerning the San Franciscan object of my affections and with my eyes still closed I reciprocated the kiss lasciviously. It was returned in kind. By the time I opened my eyes and allowed the world to come a little into focus, I found myself furiously making out with my best friend. I do not exaggerate when I say that I recoiled in horror, in the manner that two homophobic men might on finding themselves in some unexplainable compromising position. We disengaged immediately, shaking off the moment over a long run. We never spoke of the moment again, yet when I think of that one good-morning, teenagelike snog it remains in my mind's eye one of the most romantic, forbidden and charged moments in a not entirely charged life. I had, through no effort of my own, been offered exactly what I wanted and I had shrunk back, not wanting to break the spell. Needless to say, the Great Adventure was a disaster, the San Franciscan lady less than receptive to my entreaties and Angie and I drove back to Northampton in total silence, crossing the country in some forty-nine hours of nonstop driving.

Vicky was my other running partner, less given to good-morning kisses. She was also the heartbreaker to beat all heartbreakers and to walk down the street with her was to walk with a star. Were it not so wildly inappropriate, the word *stud* might fit, but in any event, we would walk down the street together and she would point out her many conquests, some smiling back, some turning away pained and others wondering what the hell she was doing with the likes of me. She mentioned her friendships, as she called them, as casually as a gardener might extol the virtues of his (or her) gardenias.

We had tried to have sex just once, but her body was too well trained to allow it; still we were, in high school terms, dating, spending all our time with each other. Occasionally she would drift into someone's arms and I would feel bereft and ridiculous. Once she spent a few days with the ex-girlfriend of one of my best male friends and there was an unhappy afternoon when this man and I sat in the park watching the two of them together across the way. We smoked and brooded and offered much bitter conjecture to each other about the nature of women who could leave men for other women. For the man who loves lesbians, lesbian sex is not enticing in the least. It is a threat to one's dearest hopes. To watch the object of your desire cavort with another woman is to feel more than unmanly, it is to feel irrelevant.

If it seems contradictory to pine for the girl one would not kiss, the girl one would not have sex with, it should. There were layers upon layers of contradictions and confusions, a sea of mismatched identities identifying with one another. Of course it was strange but it was utterly within context. Half the businesses in town appeared to be lesbian-owned, from the coffee shop where we all commiserated to the hot tub emporium and the social center for that set, a fish restaurant cum nightclub called the Northstar. It was on a date with Vicky that things began to fall apart yet further. We were at the Green Street Cafe and quite unaccountably I found myself unable to tear my eyes off our waitress. Vicky humored me for a short time, filling me in on the gossip. Courtney was the waitress's name. She was also known as a glamour dyke (she looked a little like Claudia Schiffer) and psycho, due to a public altercation with her last girlfriend that resulted in a knockout punch delivered on the dance floor of the Northstar. Presently Vicky wondered aloud if I might like to pay some attention to her instead of staring at the psycho glamour dyke. A scene developed. I didn't care about her, she said, and before I could respond Vicky had stormed out, her food untouched.

In an essay in *Esquire*, the gay writer Jonathan Van Meter posited that the 1990s is the "Post-Gay Era." His point was borne of personal experience; most of his friends had switched back and forth between gay and straight and he reasoned that after two decades of encroaching androgyny people had gotten down to liking people as opposed to genders. My own experience bore this out. My obsession had kept me firmly on the female track but most of my friends began to veer uncertainly. Courtney rather immediately settled into happy heterosexual domesticity with me and I reflect that of the three longish-term relationships I had, all three women stayed with men—a poet, a fireman and a yoga guru respectively.

By the same token, my own propensity for the gay girls began to wane. Courtney certainly had much to do with that, or rather falling in love with her did. My friends, however, remained steadfast. I moved to New York and only kept up with Kate as the months went on. She would visit every few weeks and I would half-heartedly be her beard for the evening, going to such clubs as Meow Mix and the Clit Club. She introduced me to a coterie of women called, thanks to a newspaper article, the Muffia, a group of successful womyn (publicists, club owners, musicians and the like) but I failed utterly to feel a part of things. The playfulness was not there; we were all aging, or growing up perhaps.

One evening Kate asked me, plainly, to fuck her. "To spread her legs as wide as possible and to fuck the shit out of her" was her indelicate turn of phrase. I could barely muster the enthusiasm to say no, let alone explain my rejection. I couldn't even explain it to myself. Her request had been made in the same plaintive yet icy tone as my first lesbian; everything had come full circle and I didn't want to be there anymore.

I've visited Northampton a few times since then. Everyone has dispersed, changed, grown. Some sobered up, many married their partners in genuine ceremonies. Two couples had children by means of fertilization and one of those couples decided they needed a man in the house and a woman formerly known as Karen became, quite wholly, Ken. I reflected that there ought to be another button saying *I'm a man trapped inside a lesbian's body (politic)*. Or perhaps just, *I'm a human being*.

Visions will linger, of course. At a suspiciously trendy yoga center in downtown Manhattan recently I was introduced to Ingrid Casares, the current pop-culture-friendly dyke of choice, late of Madonna's bed. Also there I bumped into a woman I'd known in Northampton, a formidable entity who'd broken Cambria's heart. She strode up to me and shook my hand firmly and I thought of the things Cambria told me she'd done with that hand and I felt the old tug of irrelevant lust, just a tinge.

Called upon to sign legislation banning lesbian sex, Queen Victoria is said to have refused on the grounds that she could not imagine what on earth women could possibly do with one another. After an immersion in the culture I have to say that I echo the Queen's sentiment. There is something mysterious and wonderful that I never could put my finger on. The space between all of us is vast enough, but between them, and for a short time between us, that space seemed much closer, less unforgiving, more welcoming.

In *A Moveable Feast,* Ernest Hemingway wrote that to live in Paris in the 1920s was to be the luckiest of men. Noting that Hemingway's talent did not begin to fly until the intervention of Gertrude Stein, I would add that Northampton in the 1990s was quite the most magical of places. I've done things backward—gazed at my cake through my twenties and only started devouring it now. I might add, in a not entirely male fashion, that it tastes better this way.

Lust and Lechery in Eight Pages: The Story of the Tijuana Bibles
Chris Hall

There is something innately pornographic about comic books. Something about the form itself, the uninhibited passion of everything from the bright, gaudy colors on dirty newsprint to the characters' exuberant declarations of heroism, villainy, love, and despair, inspires the pornographic imagination. Nothing is ever done halfway in comics, either physically or emotionally, and even the blandest books keep sexuality simmering right under the surface. Comics fans may almost universally revile his name today, but when psychiatrist Frederick Wertham asserted in his 1954 book *Seduction of the Innocent* that Batman's relationship with Robin was a homosexual fantasy and that *Wonder Woman* was a handbook for lesbian bondage, he was pretty much spot-on. You don't even need to know about the details of William Moulton Marston's very unorthodox sex life to cock an eyebrow at all the ropes and spanking that cropped up while Wonder Woman was battling the Nazis.

But sex had been an intimate part of comic books for a good ten years before Superman made his 1938 debut in *Action Comics #1*. From the 1920s to the 1950s, the first form of mass-produced pornography for thousands of Americans came in the form of crudely printed comic books called "Tijuana bibles," "eight-pagers," or simply "fuck books." The Tijuana bibles were porn in its purest form, without the slightest pretension toward art or nuance. They were not about sensuality or eroticism. They were about fucking, in a time when fucking was portrayed in no other mass medium. Tijuana bibles were created in a time before the Internet, before DVDs, before pay-per-view, before VHS or Betamax, before adult movie palaces on public streets, before a stack of *Playboy* magazines could be found in every home in America. Between the wars, the country was making the transition from nineteenth-century morals and technology to the modern age, and it did it in uneven heaves and starts. People were just getting used to the novelty of having radios, and large parts of the country wouldn't have electricity or running water until after World War II. For thousands of Americans, their first explicit images of sex, the only ones that were regularly available to them, were the thin, cheap pages of the Tijuana bibles.

The typical Tijuana bible was eight pages long in a four by three format in black-and-white, or sometimes red or blue and white ink. Some bibles were sixteen pages long, and a few very extravagant ones even reached the mammoth size of thirty-two pages. One of the ironies of time is that virtually the only comics distributed today that are similar in size and shape to the Tijuana bibles are the Christian tracts that Jack Chick has drawn and sold for the last thirty-nine years. The content and philosophy of Chick's work is 180 degrees away from that of the fuck books, if no less extreme in its passion and fantasy. In Chick's world, teenagers get sucked into black magic and human sacrifice by the temptations of Dungeons and Dragons or Christian rock bands, and the Catholic Church lurks behind endless conspiracies ranging from the Holocaust to the rise of Islam.

While Chick has used the format to plead with his readers to turn from earthly sin and embrace Jesus, the world of the Tijuana bibles vigorously indulged carnal pleasures in every combination that could possibly be squeezed into eight narrow pages. The characters in those pages were invariably familiar, even if their behavior wasn't. Every icon of popular culture—from comic strip characters to movie stars and even politicians—ultimately found themselves starring in at least one of the bibles. Within the pages of the Tijuana bibles, Mickey and Minnie's relationship was finally consummated; Josef Stalin serviced the proletariat in ways Marx never imagined; and Jimmy Cagney fellated Pat O'Brien. As well as being the predecessors of today's slash fiction, the Tijuana bibles provide a secret history of popular culture at the time. Every well-loved comic character, every movie star who made hearts throb and laps moist, at some time found their corporate-enforced chastity peeled away to expose inelegant and insatiable lusts.

The sexuality the Tijuana bibles depicted was not beautiful. It wasn't nuanced enough to be considered "erotic." It was frequently not only crude but also hateful and ugly. Reading the bibles today, one can't help but be impressed by how they are so obviously a product of a sexually repressive society, where discussion of sexuality—and especially sexuality's pleasures—was all but excluded from the public square. The erotic charge of the bibles seems to depend on the sexual naïveté of the reader; underlying all of them is a sense of amazement that such a thing as sex even exists. To captivate their audience, they had to do little more that simply acknowledge cocks, tits, cunts and asses.

But, of course, there was more to the bibles. After all, it wasn't just anyone's genitalia on display in those pages. By the 1930s, newspaper comics were already big business. William Randolph Hearst and Joseph Pulitzer fought near-epic struggles over the strips and creators, and the decades-long war between the two helped elevate the art form to its creative and commercial zenith. The most popular characters were merchandised as toys and on clothing and found new life in other media. E. C. Segar's salty, spinach-eating sailor Popeye virtually became a cottage industry after he debuted in 1929; starting in the 1930s, Popeye gave his stamp of approval to almost everything that could be sold, and starred in many classic animated shorts by the Fleischer Brothers studio. Chic Young's *Blondie* and Chester Gould's *Dick Tracy* were not only iconic in their print forms but also thrived in their adaptations to radio and film. The characters from all three strips—and others—quickly became shorthand for very specific traits and personalities. Americans knew them. When the country was first being crushed by economic depression followed by the destruction of war, they *were* America, in the best sense we could imagine.

And then they were stripped naked in the pages of the Tijuana bibles. Looking through the bibles has the same forbidden kick as if you happened to wander past the window of a beloved neighbor just in time to see her hungrily sucking off Pastor Ted and getting rimmed by your Aunt Sally. It's not just anyone in these comic books. If it were, it's hard to imagine that they'd get anything more than cursory attention by a few comics historians known for being die-hard completists.

Look, for example, at the mix of class and sexual anxieties

in the Blondie and Dagwood eight-pager "Fired!" In terms of art quality and storytelling skill, this one represents the bibles at their very lowest. Dagwood's cantankerous boss, Mr. Dithers (here called Smithers), is barely recognizable, and the spelling and layout are elementary at best. The sex scenes look like they were drawn by a boy still wondering what girls look like under their dresses. It's exactly the sort of thing that you probably drew in the back of your fifth-grade English class.

But despite the distorted art and the crudely pornographic story, "Fired!" doesn't seem that far removed from Chic Young's daily strip. Right in the first panel, Dagwood once again gets his lazy ass canned by Smithers, a gag that even the most casual reader of the original knows. He goes home and rants to Blondie about "that prick Smithers," but instead of being merely passive and comforting, by page three Blondie is in Smithers' office demanding Dagwood's job back. Almost immediately, Smithers starts groping Blondie's twat despite her protests. By page five, sexual assault is transformed into impassioned demands for Smithers to fuck her harder and deeper. At last, Dagwood appears on the scene; looking more put out than outraged, he jerks his cock while watching his boss screw his wife, petulantly complaining, "At least you could let me get in." Smithers keeps pumping away, responding nastily, "Shut up Bumstead you got your job back what more do you want." The narration observes without pity, "Looks like Dagwoods the on who got fucked." [sic]

Alongside its crude sexual fantasy, "Fired!" injects the tired gags of *Blondie* with realities that the strip studiously avoided. The lecherous boss held real power in the 1930s, enabled by a lack of sexual harassment laws and economic desperation. And anyone watching Dagwood's constant firings has to wonder why Blondie tolerates it in such precarious times. Blondie's aggressive response to Dithers/Smithers here is much more plausible. Even the Bumsteads' lascivious appetites seem much more in character when you consider the origins of the strip, which chronicled the adventures of a flapper named Blondie Boopadoop, who loved the dance halls and parties of the 1920s but eventually fell for Dagwood, the dissolute scion of the upper-crust Bumsteads. When the two married, Dagwood's parents cut him off without a cent for disgracing the family by marrying a working-class trollop.

Dagwood's humiliation is another common feature of the bibles. They catered to the sexual fears of their readers as much as they did their fantasies, and a common theme is the sexual humiliation or defeat of the protagonist. In "Bigger Yet," starring "Claudette Coal-Bin," a delivery boy who's been lucky enough to get laid by the great movie star gets kicked out on his ass on page eight, his cock still rock hard, when he makes the slip of telling her that his boss is even bigger than he is. In "Chris Crusty VII," the protagonist winds up getting beaten and robbed when the woman's husband comes home; the last page shows him telling a flirtatious young woman to "go pound sand up yer ass!!!" In a nasty display of misogyny and anti-Semitism, "Gimme Beck" portrays Geezil, a caricatured Jew from the early Popeye strips, unsatisfied by what he gets for his five dollars from a hooker. In retaliation, he slips his fingers inside her and declares, "Ah dot's it!! Now listen you bedroom boiglar!! I'm the boss—one finger I got up your ass and my thumb in your cunt—now, give it beck my five bucks or I rip out the partition!"

The history of the Tijuana bibles is largely speculation, the creators unknown. You can say the same about much of comics history, but the bibles were actually illegal, whereas *Superman* and *Millie the Model* were merely disreputable and juvenile. Even the origins of the name are uncertain. The bibles didn't come from Mexico, but because many people picked them up in border towns, it could have been the specific reputation of Tijuana for forbidden pleasures, or it could have been outright racism. For whatever reason, the name stuck.

Even though the bibles violated virtually every obscenity law in the United States, that inhibited their production and distribution no more than Prohibition kept Americans from getting ahold of gin. Between seven hundred and one thousand titles were published from the '30s to the '50s. In *The Tijuana Bibles: America's Forgotten Comic Strips,* comic historian R. C. Harvey cites a 1992 paper by Robert Gluckson that estimated that in 1939 alone, three hundred titles were produced with a total of three million copies. "Other sources," Harvey writes, "say twenty million copies were produced yearly by the end of the decade." Whatever the numbers say, though, they're just broad guesses. The artists, printers, and distributors took great pains not to leave records of how much and what they produced.

The term *underground* has pretty much been diminished to a marketing gimmick to make middle-class consumers feel transgressive. In the days of the Tijuana bibles, though, underground networks were the only way to buy or sell them without legal consequences. Harvey describes the course taken by the bibles as "drawn in attics, printed in garages on cantankerous machinery, and distributed surreptitiously from the back pockets of shady vendors in alleyways and in dimly lit rooms." Occasionally, organized crime was involved in the manufacture and distribution, but even at their height, no mobster was going to become a major player by selling twenty-five-cent fuck books. Despite the mass quantity that Gluckson and others estimate, selling bibles was a small-time racket.

The names of the creators have been almost entirely lost to

history. One of the few exceptions to this rule was dubbed "Mr. Prolific" by Donald H. Gilmore in his work *Sex in Comics*. The prophetically named sexologist Gershon Legman eventually identified Mr. Prolific as "Doc" Rankin, a World War I veteran who worked for Larch Publications, a publisher of girlie cartoons and dirty joke books, in the 1930s. Art Spiegelman unabashedly praised Rankin's work as he would a respected colleague in the introduction to Bob Adelman's anthology *Tijuana Bibles:* "He was not only the seminal influence on the genre, he was by far its most competent draftsman, drawing credible likenesses in complex entangled poses with graceful steel-pen strokes. This guy was good enough to earn an honest living had he so desired. Visibly enjoying his work, he offered good value, often adding extra gags and caricatures in frames inside the frames."

Spiegelman assigns a moniker of his own to one of the post-War artists: Mr. Dyslexic. Spiegelman's judgment of Mr. Dyslexic is as harsh and merciless as his praise of Rankin is effusive: "He has no sense of left-to-right narrative progression and is constantly placing his figures or his balloons (and sometimes both) out of sequence. By hidden example he teaches the hidden difficulties of the cartoonist's craft. He can't draw even rudimentarily well, certainly can't spell, and holds for me as a working cartoonist the same fascination a really nasty car accident might hold for a bus driver." Mr. Dyslexic's failings as an artist are visible even to an untrained eye, and while he certainly deserves every iota of wrath that Spiegelman calls down upon him, it has to be said that his work never reached the depths of incompetence shown in "Fired!" One of his works, "Chambers and Hiss in Betrayed," is fascinating for the way it blends obscenity with Cold War paranoia. The 1948 Chambers-Hiss case remains one of the most contentious and emblematic of post-War political divisions.

Whittaker Chambers, a Communist Party member, testified before the House Un-American Activities Committee (HUAC) that State Department official Alger Hiss was a Soviet spy. Until the collapse of the Soviet Union (and to an extent, even today), whether you believed Hiss or Chambers was seen as representing where you stood on broader issues. Mr. Dyslexic explains Chambers and Hiss by imagining a sexual affair between the two. Hiss unforgivably betrays his lover with a woman, leading Chambers to turn Hiss over to the Feds. "I'll not have him," Chambers says as Hiss is led away in cuffs, "but neither will any woman."

The Trouble with Safe Sex
Seth Michael Donsky

It's Friday night, and I'm headed to the East Side Club, one of the last two remaining gay bathhouses in New York City.

Ostensibly a relaxation and social club for gay and bisexual men, it's located on two floors of a nondescript office building on East 58th Street. I take an elevator to the sixth floor and wait behind a thick, Plexiglas window in a dark cell of a foyer, reminiscent of a vintage, blue movie theater box office. Posters for events such as the International Mr. Leather Contest, prominently featuring half-naked men, line the walls.

After a few moments, the manager buzzes me in through a small door. I am immediately overcome by a smell of chlorine, industrial-strength disinfectant, locker-room funk and poppers.

A labyrinth of interconnecting dark hallways is lined on either side with innumerable clapboard rooms. Each room contains a twin-sized cot, a hook for hanging your clothes and a table with a couple of condoms and a packet of lube. But whether anyone will be using the provided protection is anyone's guess.

The lights in each room are on a dimmer but, as none of the rooms have ceilings, ambient light and noise easily spill over from the hallway. It's here in the hallway that I meet Rubin.

A slim, youthful-looking Filipino, Rubin's soft, delicate features belie the fact that he's actually thirty-seven years old. He blushes when he admits that, in sexual trysts, he often lets men his own age believe that he's many years their junior.

When I question him, he explains to me that he had been getting tested regularly for HIV every six months since coming out at age twenty and moving to New York City. Those tests stopped two years ago, however, after a night of heavy drinking when he had "bareback" sex with his best friend of fourteen years, an HIV-positive man.

Bareback sex is a popular and, in its implied rebellion, erotic term within the gay community for sex without a condom. Rubin has been vaguely unsettled by that high-risk incident and does not talk about HIV status with the men he hooks up with. He knows he could have sought HIV testing and counseling if he had really wanted to, but part of what has stood in the way is his shame.

"I'm afraid that people will tell me I should have known better," he explains, casting his soft, brown eyes toward the ground. "That I did this to myself. I just don't want to hear that."

Tonight, Rubin has decided to get an HIV test. He's getting it here, in the middle of a sex club. Wearing nothing but a towel, he chats with me after having had his blood drawn.

"I don't think these people are judging me," he says of Dr. Demetre Daskalakis, director of the Men's Sexual Health Project (MSHP, pronounced "Em-Ship"), the diagnostic center inside the club where the testing is administered. "I mean, how could they? Look where we are. And besides, he's cute," Rubin says of Mike Dreyden, the porn star who's promoting tonight's testing. "I've never met a porn star before," he admits. "And I want the DVD." In addition to raffling off his latest release (the proceeds go to MSHP), Dreyden is giving away a free DVD sampler of porn previews to anyone who gets tested.

It's been more than twenty-five years since the publication of Richard Berkowitz and Michael Callen's brochure, "How to Have Sex in an Epidemic," introduced the notion of "safe sex." Most gay men know the message by now, but the safe-sex rhetoric no longer seems to be working. At least it's no longer producing the intended behavior. In fact, it may be producing a whole slew of new behaviors that work to defeat the message.

The fact that sex without condoms feels better—both physically and often emotionally—is an intense temptation. Many gay men—in fact, most men, regardless of sexual preference—want to have sex without condoms and, sooner or later, most do.

Recently released reports from both the CDC in Atlanta and the New York City Department of Health confirm that new HIV infection rates are rising dramatically in certain key demographics, particularly in young men (in their teens and twenties) and men of color, both locally and nationally, even as overall rates are in decline. And those numbers don't take into account the infected and at-risk individuals who aren't getting tested or counseled. Additionally, other sexually transmitted diseases, such as syphilis, which were once almost wiped out are now on the rise again—a sign of risky behaviors.

The safe-sex message was born at a time of crisis when HIV was a literal death sentence. Since then, radical changes in disease treatment have (hopefully and optimistically) turned HIV into a chronic, rather than fatal, condition. An entire generation of sexually active young men now exists that wasn't even in existence when the crisis was at its peak. Plus, legions of men who have practiced using condoms for most of their lives are beginning to seriously wonder what they've been missing.

One of the least-discussed developments is the fact that some men live a lifestyle where they not only prefer, but insist upon, sex without condoms. And now some of these "barebackers" have started calling bareback sex "natural sex," implying that it is the safe sexers who are engaged in unnatural behavior by wearing condoms.

The only response we have to these developments, however, is the same, tired message: safe sex. The implied judgment of that message is that smart people always use a condom and so those who choose not to, for whatever reason, likely feel shame.

Dr. Daskalakis, who received specialized medical training on HIV in Boston, at Harvard Medical School and Massachusetts General Hospital, before founding MSHP in 2006, concedes that shame is a big part of why it's so difficult for us to talk about sex.

"I love working with commercial sex venues, and would never say anything bad about them," he says. "But why do they exist? One reason is that people think it's hot to have sex with a lot of people in one place. The other reason I think, frankly, is shame. I feel like the way that we push sex—gay sex in particular, and unprotected gay sex especially—into this place of badness, whether it's pathologized because of HIV and STDs, or pathologized because of some moral majority, I think what that automatically creates is shame and the need to hide what you're doing. I feel like shame is still a major part of what is going on in the community."

The shame implied by the safe-sex message makes it difficult for HIV-positive people to disclose their status or to talk openly and honestly about their medical challenges.

Dr. Richard Greene, a frequent volunteer with MSHP, tells of a med school student in his twenties who called him after a sexual encounter with a man who revealed his HIV-positive status afterward. The young student was shaken and wanted Dr. Greene's advice as to when or how or if to inquire about HIV in regard to having sex. "And this is a med school student," says Dr. Greene. "How is the average guy supposed to know how to deal with this?"

It's 9:00 p.m. on a Friday, still relatively early by bathhouse standards. Nevertheless, approximately five dozen men—of various shapes and sizes, skin color and ages (a good portion of whom appear to be in their fifties and sixties)—draped only in towels, walk back and forth in a never-ending, circuitous parade.

It's a solemn ritual whereby potential sexual partners scope each other out and express and deflect interest by the subtlest of gestures: a quick nod, a knowing glance, a grab of the crotch or briskly brushing up against one another.

MSHP, an affiliation between Bellevue Hospital and the NYU School of Medicine, under Dr. Daskalakis's direction, provides free HIV and STD testing inside this club and the West Side Club, the other remaining gay bathhouse in New York City, on a rotating schedule. The organization also recently offered HIV and STD testing inside the annual Black Party, a well-attended, sexually charged circuit party that takes place at Roseland Ballroom. It is a far more euphoric setting than the West or East Side clubs.

"Working at the Black Party was amazing," Dr. Daskalakis tells me later, when I follow up after the infamous bacchanal. "We tested higher than our capacity given staffing and space, proving that HIV prevention should work with nightlife and not against it."

MSHP's mission is to bring accurate information about HIV and STDs to sexually active men who have sex with men and to connect them with care. Dreyden, the porn star, discovered MSHP's booth at the 2008 Gay Erotic Expo where, incidentally, he happened to be the poster boy for the event.

He was so impressed that MSHP was offering testing and counseling where sex was happening that he wanted to use his porn-star cachet to support it in whatever way he could: he decided to promote HIV testing by giving away porn instead of condoms. The collaboration may be the most culturally significant thing to come out of a gay bathhouse since Bette Midler and Barry Manilow played the Continental Baths.

Dreyden's mother was a Registered Medical Assistant who didn't shy away from frank, open discussions about sexuality with him and his sister while they were growing up. He says he's impressed by the range of services available to HIV-positive people (he, himself, is HIV-negative), but he thinks there is a lack of services available for people who aren't sure of their status and are afraid to get tested.

"Every time I get tested, it freaks me the fuck out. I play safe. I know I'm okay," he explains. "But going in, filling out the paperwork, hearing about the worst-case scenario; it freaks me out. I don't think straight people have to deal with anything quite like this."

Dreyden is reacting to the need for a more nuanced message. The safe-sex message may have worked when the "penalty" was death, but it has proven less effective now.

Perhaps the lack of an evolved message can be blamed on eight years of flat funding for the National Institutes of Health under the Bush administration, making little money available for educational outreach, or the CDC funding only abstinence-based initiatives, rendering what little outreach was offered ineffective. Or accuse HIV medication advertising for minimizing the consequences of the disease.

Whatever the reason, the stakes for new infections have never been higher and, without a new message that addresses the reality of bareback sex, those rates are likely to continue to increase.

The culture of bareback sex is one of the most fascinating consequences of twenty-five years of the safe-sex message.

"What we suppress, expresses," explains author, lecturer and sex educator Barbara Carrellas (www.urbantantra.org). She, like Dr. Daskalakis, was inspired to become a sex educator in response to the great loss of life and health in the original wave of the HIV epidemic. "If you study the course of what has been a fetish over time, you discover that the essential badness and kinkiness associated with something is an integral part of the fetish."

"The bareback community," explains Max Sohl, a NYC-based producer/director for Treasure Island Media, one of the first exclusively bareback porn production companies, "is defined by men who have made the decision to seek out 'natural sex' and are not afraid of it. This is different from men who are practicing safe sex but 'slip up' for one reason or another…or men who are barebacking with their partners but practicing safe sex with men outside their relationship."

This important distinction is most evident in the world of gay, bareback porn. Few people consider "vintage," or pre-condom porn (porn made before the HIV crisis, mostly in the 1970s and '80s) bareback porn, even though the performers don't use condoms. It isn't the lack of condoms alone that makes porn, or sex for that matter, bareback. It is the conscious lack of condoms in the face of the safe-sex message that generates the essential "badness," the excitement and the fetish.

"I believe," continues Sohl, "that the labeling of 'bareback' porn is a creation of the gay community. What I do is document real men having real sex—that sex just happens to not involve the use of condoms. When I started working with Treasure Island in 2003, you couldn't find a bareback video in any store in New York City."

Sohl notes that adult video stores now stock huge sections of the formerly illicit material. "It went from being a taboo, underground, fetish genre with a niche audience," says Sohl, "to topping the gay DVD charts in sales and rentals."

It's not just in porn; a random sampling of several online sex hook-up sites (including Craigslist M4M personals)—filtered for key words such as "bareback," "BB" and "raw"—turns up dozens of listings. Few of them mention HIV status.

Even *GAYVN* (pronounced "Gay Vee Enn"), the industry magazine that covers gay porn and hosts one of the most highly visible porn awards ceremonies, has had to make concessions to bareback's growing popularity. Up until very recently, the company had not acknowledged bareback porn or allowed any of the bareback movies to be nominated for awards. But a recent switch in management to a new editorial staff that believes its job is to document the trends in gay porn without moralizing and pressure from the advertising department to sell ad space to bareback companies has changed that.

"We have to contend with it," says *GAYVN* editor-in-chief Harker Jones. "Bareback porn is no longer a fad." *GAYVN* tried, in 2008, to create and implement a set of what they considered responsible standards (such as mandatory STD testing) by which bareback porn companies could become eligible for award nominations this year. But the landscape became too difficult to navigate, and the venture was abandoned.

Shame and fear of judgment is also what makes it difficult for HIV-negative people to ask their physicians serious questions about the risks of unprotected sex or for physicians to know how to properly respond.

Tyler, an acquaintance of mine, revealed that he often engaged in sex without condoms. His recollection of the conversations he would have with his doctor, a physician with a large gay practice, prior to seroconverting (becoming HIV-positive), are disturbing.

"He would ask me if I was using condoms all the time, and I would say, 'No,' and he would say, 'Well, you should.' And I would say, 'I know,' and that was that."

The unfortunate result, then, is that most people only learn the real consequences of seroconversion after they have converted, and it's too late to make an informed choice.

Since seroconverting, Tyler has become an avowed barebacker. He loves having sex without a condom. He has performed in bareback porn, he escorts and only uses condoms at the direct request of clients (he never offers), and he is currently in an open relationship in which he and his boyfriend almost exclusively insist on bareback sex with other men. They rarely disclose their status (both positive) and are almost never asked. Tyler has also maintained a healthy T-cell count, so it would appear the consequences haven't been so dire.

So, I asked him whether the "privilege" of being able to have all the bareback sex he wanted outweighed the disadvantages of having HIV. "No," he said, "definitely not. It's a booby prize. I'd rather have my health."

"Doctors think they know that people with HIV are going to live, hopefully, happier, healthier, longer lives, with maybe a few extra pitfalls along the way," says Dr. Daskalakis, "but that's based on conjecture. We haven't yet had a generation of people with HIV living full, average life expectancies. Serious medical complications are likely to develop, and side effects from the meds can be severe and debilitating in their own right. Even under the best of circumstances, an HIV diagnosis means that you are likely to have to see a doctor regularly for the rest of your life and all that entails."

Shame often compels people to act in secret. Later at the West Side Club, I spoke with Chris, another MSHP test client. He is an unassuming guy in his early thirties with a wholesome, Broadway chorus boy look about him. He's supposedly been in a monogamous relationship for four years but has repeatedly had bareback sex outside of the relationship. Although he has recently come clean to his boyfriend about the sex—and has entered a 12-step program for sexual compulsion—he hasn't been able to admit to his partner that the sex he had was not safe. "I'm afraid of his reaction. I mean, I put his life at risk."

Shame also drives some people to lie. Keith seroconverted in what he understood to be a monogamous relationship and, to this day, his ex-boyfriend claims to be HIV-negative. Keith did have sex with a few other men toward the end of his relationship, so he admits he might have been exposed then, but what little sex he had outside of the relationship was safe. He only barebacked with his boyfriend. "I remember once seeing what I thought was an STD on him, but he denied it. I mean where would it have come from? We were monogamous. Sometimes I wonder." Keith has gone to the other end of the spectrum and now insists on disclosure and wearing condoms. "But I see guys online on hook-up sites all the time," he says, "who list themselves as HIV-negative when I know for a fact that they are HIV-positive because we've disclosed to each other and had sex. For a fact."

It appears people simply aren't getting and sharing the information they need to make informed choices about their lives and their health. Knowing your HIV status is only the first step.

"Make no assumptions about anything," says Carrellas. "Do not assume that people hold the same values as you or even define something in the same way you do. Not even monogamy. People can have vastly different interpretations."

Carrellas proposes a model along the lines of safe, sane, consensual, risk-aware sex in place of the safe-sex message. "It's a model from the kink world," she explains, "whereby someone can say I am aware of certain risks and I am willing to play with this much risk, but not that much risk. Gay men were the sexual adventurers of the twentieth century, and they had some great skills prior to HIV. Negotiation was one of them. You really had to know how to negotiate back then if you wanted to play with the leather boys. You had to be able to name your desires, set your limits and talk about it. We could use a return to some of those truly queer roots."

Carrellas is talking about honest, genuine sexual negotiation. "We may not all be able to agree on how safe we want to be collectively," she says. "But if we can't agree on being safe, sane and consensual with the people we are playing with, we're in real trouble."

It's the minimum we should expect. Everyone is entitled to make informed choices about their lives and take the associated risks they are comfortable with in their own pursuit of happiness. And we're not simply talking about the health risks that HIV-negative people assume in the absence of negotiation.

HIV-positive people also assume great psychological risk when they lie or misrepresent themselves to potential sexual partners. It's bad enough when people make decisions without being adequately informed or aware of the degree of risk they are assuming. But when the best available public message about that risk is not strong enough to overcome the attraction of the behavior and, worse, actually generates the sorts of feelings and behaviors that keep accurate information underground, it's a genuine tragedy.

One of Dr. Daskalakis's goals with MSHP is to facilitate dialogue among and between men who have sex with men who are not necessarily socially connected and to integrate those men into the larger community.

"It's always the 'dirty dog' that goes to the bathhouses and causes a problem," says Dr. Daskalakis. "But that dirty dog is often married and has children. The complexity of this is so great that anything we can do to bring it into the light, anything, we should."

That brings me back to where I started, the middle of the East Side Club on a Friday night, talking to Rubin. He's stepped away to get his results and his free porn sampler and to ask whatever questions he has of Dr. Daskalakis and his staff. It's a good twenty minutes before he learns his result. He's negative.

Rubin recedes back into the dim hallway and takes his place in the ritual dance surrounding us—one more anonymous face.

What he does with this new information is up to him. As it should be.

Piece of Ass
Monica Shores

It was my fault for bringing up the sex toy for dogs. In retrospect, that was what started it all. But what else should I have responded with when one of Brian's cats jumped on the back of the couch and began laying her claws and teeth into my hair in what can only be described as a near-abusive seduction?

"Wow, look at her go," Stacey said, wineglass in hand. "Peaches, you better calm down." Calming down, however, was the last thing the cat had in mind. She kneaded aggressively as her purring increased.

"It's okay," I said. I tried to ignore the fact that a pet was perched on my head in front of two strangers who repeatedly claimed they wanted me in their bed. "Cats just really like my hair."

It was ten o'clock on a Wednesday night and we were in Brian's apartment, the three of us down to our underwear on a couch in front of a coffee table sporting several empty bottles. Stacey was crouching against the armrest to my left, I was poised tensely in the middle, and Brian was reclining on my right, legs splayed and fingertips dangling over my shoulder near my breast. This was our second attempt at a threesome. The first had ended, to Brian's transparent disappointment, on another week night when I said moving to the bedroom was up to Stacey, and Stacey pointed out that it was already two and she had work in the morning. She and Brian had been dating for six months and, according to Brian, were "not serious."

"You know…" I began as Peaches continued her scalp-molestation, which neither Brian nor Stacey seem particularly interested in stopping, "they make sex dolls for dogs. Just little plastic things that the dog can mount."

"I think I've seen those," Stacey said. She was topless and in cotton panties, her hair pulled into a ponytail. I'd worn a matching black lace set, and felt painfully overdressed, although the cat-styled hair was mitigating that concern.

"I actually sort of, ah—I sort of have something like that. A toy." Brian grinned boyishly, faux embarrassed. He bounced his knee against mine.

"For Peaches? I don't think it's working," I said.

"No, for me."

"What, like a blow-up doll? Did someone give it to you as a joke?" I asked.

"It doesn't blow up," Stacey said. She stared at Brian with a look I couldn't decipher.

"A Fleshlight?" I tried again. I sat up straight, and Peaches finally abandoned my hair. "A Real Doll?"

"No. It's not a whole body, it's just…" Brian gestured with his hands, keeping up the naughty boy act. "Just her, you know, lower part." Earlier, he'd expressed pride that people sometimes referred to him as "Ken Doll." He was lanky and tan with spiky blond hair; Stacey was equally blonde and tan, sans spikes. Perhaps it was only fitting that he had a literal doll partner as well as a real-life Barbie-esque one.

"She has a name," Stacey said. "Megan. After Megan Fox. She's very lifelike."

"Oh…" This development was even more stymieing than the amorous cat. The coffee table candles were starting to gutter. I noticed an open package of Twizzlers amid the magazines and remotes. I hadn't imagined my first threesome unfolding this way. But it was. Finally I said, "Well, can I see it?"

Megan was, in fact, impressively lifelike. Stacey and I lay side by side on the bed as I examined her. She was made of Cyberskin, or something denser, spongy yet firm, smooth, and slightly tacky to the touch. When Brian tossed her on the bed, she fell heavily, like a giant slab of thawed meat. She was almost all undercarriage, cut off at the low belly and flat on the backside. There were the beginnings of inner thighs, and her bare pubis was surrounded by realistic goose bumps, just like the mildly irritated texture of most girls' bikini area when they shave. Her vulva was very pretty, with flowery, soft lips, and below her tiny vaginal opening was an even tinier asshole. The anatomy was actually spaced properly. It was as though she were spreading her legs wide and lifting up her pelvis, tilting it to show off her little orifices. Saucy girl.

"She has no clit," I pointed out, distressed. It seemed tremendously perverse that she would be made so detailed and yet not given her greatest source of pleasure. (Perverse, yet entirely predictable given the sex industry's understanding of female orgasms.)

"I think the bigger problem is that she doesn't have a brain," Brian said, joining us on the bed. "Let's get her a head before we worry about her clit." Then, reconsidering, "Or some tits."

"So, you watch him use it?" I said to Stacey. "I don't even know how he fits in." Brian had taken off his shorts while fetching Megan, once again confirming my theory about tall men and their commensurate appendages.

"Sometimes she watches," Brian answered. He began stroking my thigh, affecting a casual air.

"Sometimes I hold her open for him," Stacey demonstrated spreading the fake flesh with her hands. This disturbed me to an unreasonable degree, as though she were detailing a rape. "But we also play with her together."

Of course. As if her helping him use it wasn't bizarre enough. I had to ask, "How do you use it together?"

They exchanged glances. "Well," Brian was firmly back in coy mode. "When we play with her…Megan is you."

I didn't follow up with any questions this time. I suppose it should have been flattering that they'd integrated me into their sex life during the very brief time we'd known each other. I'm a brunette, too, so it wasn't as though Megan's namesake and I had nothing in common.

But I couldn't enjoy whatever ego boost Brian's comment was intended to provide. I was too overwhelmed with images of Stacey licking the plastic non-clit while Brian was plunging into Megan, or Stacey fingering Megan's miniature hole while trying to thrust backward against Brian. I was a little grossed out, yet intrigued. I considered asking for a demonstration, but Brian had put his hand on the back of my head and was guiding my face toward Stacey's. I kissed her, parting my lips and putting my hand on her thigh. Her lips were closed in an exaggerated pucker, as though we were once-removed relatives.

Brian insisted that Stacey was into girls, and that, more relevantly, she was into me. The chemistry between him and me wasn't an issue. From the moment he'd rolled open his yoga mat next to mine, I was game for pretty much anything he would propose. After the first meeting between the three of us, a text was sent from Stacey's phone saying I was hot and that she couldn't wait to get naked with me, even though she seemed practically asexual during the two hours we'd all spent talking. I assumed she was just nervous. She wasn't entirely clueless when it came to girl-on-girl scenarios. She corrected me when I called tribbing "scissoring" instead of its apparently more proper term.

Part of the second evening's early foreplay, which in retrospect might have been advance warning of the Megan revelation, involved Brian and Stacey going through *Hustler* spreads and pointing out which girl was supposed to be me and which one was supposed to be Stacey. There was something childlike and goofy about all of it, reminiscent of when girls assign themselves and their friends personalities from cartoons like "The Powerpuff Girls," or "Sex and the City." It wasn't hot but it was a little endearing, and I had gone along with it. After all, these were two very good-looking people. Maybe this was what all conventionally attractive couples were like in bed. This was a learning experience for me.

But for all this professed girl-lust, Stacey kept her kisses chaste. When I commented that I loved her breasts, she said something about wanting to lose ten pounds. Ryan unhooked my bra, perhaps hoping she would return the compliment, and instead she said, "I think Megan might be jealous." As much as a fake vulva can bear witness, Megan was indeed still on the bed, "watching," where she stayed for at least an hour. In the confusion of constantly negotiating three bodies, I occasionally felt my knee land squarely on her squishy lips, or realized my hand was jammed against her almost-thigh. But I always adjusted myself, not her. Although they weren't attending to her at the moment, she seemed too integral to Brian and Stacey's sex life for me to interfere. When Brian finally tossed her to the floor, he did so with a "Sorry, Megan, but you've got to go." Stacey echoed him sadly: "Sorry, Megan."

Hours later, the three of us collapsed, sticky and red-faced and sweaty. Brian put his arm around Stacey's shoulder. "That was amazing," he said, and began laughing in delight. Stacey stared at the ceiling. She'd kept her eyes shut for much of what had just taken place, except for one particularly charged moment when she'd caught me deep-throating Brian. I say "caught" because I'd felt like a sex criminal once she saw me. What her eyes telegraphed was not appreciation or arousal or any of the other emotions you might hope to find while in a threesome, but simply shock verging on anger. I had transgressed, done something too intimate or too unusual—something Megan would never have done.

"Uh, yeah...I better get home," I said, lying away from them in my own island of messy sheets.

"Okay," Stacey replied. While I was putting on my sneakers, she threw out a surprisingly maternal, "Let us know you got home safe," from behind the couch, ten feet from the front door. Brian kissed my cheek good-bye in the foyer.

Over the next few days, I was bombarded with messages from Brian asking when could we do it again, wasn't it the most incredible night ever, and what was my favorite part? I finally wrote him a diplomatic email detailing that, while they were both great people, I didn't think I was Stacey's taste. He vehemently denied it.

She loved it, he texted me. *We talk about it all the time.*

I didn't reply, and eventually he wrote, *She'll be sending you a message herself.* As promised, I did get a text from Stacey about a day later, which ended with *Maybe we shall do it again sometime.* Brian had texted me an hour earlier asking if I was free that evening. They might have spent a lot of time talking, but they didn't spend much time listening.

My time with Brian and Stacey was unsatisfying in a way I didn't understand. I wasn't a stranger to casual sex and I didn't feel responsible for their miscommunication. It was something trickier than that. I wanted to blame it on their penchant for the pornographic, their obsession with choreographing each moment to mimic a magazine spread instead of just letting things feel good. Even Stacey's orgasms were treated like interference. At one point, she bleated out, "Came!" and immediately returned to fingering herself. Nothing was savored. Nothing flowed.

After a week of unanswered pleas to recreate the threesome, Brian sent me a message telling me he was alone and I should come over. I considered it. I thought about his flat stomach and shaved chest, of the tone he'd achieved all along his body so that one expanse of flesh hardly felt different from another. I thought maybe it would be better with him and me alone, without Stacey's lukewarm lesbianism to get in our way. And, god willing, without Megan.

Then I realized I couldn't recall the feel of his skin under my hands. Had I once touched him anywhere besides his cock? I couldn't remember what it felt like when he touched me. I couldn't even remember where he touched me. The threesome was a blur not because it was a steady stream of pleasure but because it was empty, with no memorable moments to cling to. And if Brian had been posing and Stacey playacting, it was because I allowed it and had done the same with them. That night, we had all been like children with dolls. I didn't want to play that game again.

The Future of Sex Ed
Violet Blue

Let's just get this part of the discussion out of the way: I'm not even going to pretend that John McCain has a broken condom of a chance at a term in the Oval Office. Barack Obama is going to be our next president, and our next first lady is going to be the coolest grande dame in United States history. The first couple, incidentally, is going to burn up the presidential bed.

The Obamas are a hot and cool couple, and they seem to be more in touch with the real world outside of D.C. than any presidential couple to hit the White House sheets. But Barack's going to have to don a hazmat suit and a full-body condom to even begin to clean up the mess he's inheriting. Iraq, for starters. But let's not forget about the children, shall we? You know, the ones getting pregnant and contracting STDs at jaw-dropping rates and at younger ages than previous generations in spite of…perhaps, even because of federally funded (read: "state strong-armed") abstinence education. In which "education" should always be in quotes.

Recently I was at Philz Coffee with a nineteen-year-old friend who grew up in the South Bay. He was telling me about the sex ed he very recently got in high school. They separated the genders (um, that's another column). The principal brought in a locked—locked!—briefcase with tapes (tapes!). The students watched cartoons about reproduction and puberty, and that was that. He told me, "It was so dumb. Everyone already knew that stuff. It didn't tell us anything about what we were all really doing." I asked him where kids went to get their questions answered. He said, "Well, I went to your website."

Good thing he's nineteen. But recently in Australian schools, researchers put together a groundbreaking sexual health program for sixteen- to twenty-five-year-olds. Associate Professor Moira Carmody from the University of Western Sydney's Social Justice and Social Change Research Centre did something totally shocking: she asked teens what they needed from their sex-ed programs. Carmody interviewed young people about their sexual activity, experiences and concerns. Instead of telling them that sex is bad or sinful or that you can catch AIDS from a public library computer someone once used to look at porn, she used the kids' feedback to create a six-week program, subsequently run in six communities in Sydney and regional New South Wales.

That's quite a bit different than what our federal government pressures public schools to tell kids—and this is certainly where Obama should be taking notes. Like I said last year, abstinence education is a failure, but at the eleventh hour of 2007 it still got a huge pile of federal cash. In most American public schools it focuses exclusively on reproduction and marriage, and only shows students illustrations. Abstinence has always been taught on one level or another, but when George W. took office, an "abstinence-only" focus was aggressively pushed as the primary—the only—way to give kids information about sex.

Here, no one asks kids what they're experiencing and what information they could use to help navigate decision-making in sexual situations. What's worse, according to the curriculum content guidelines for funding recipients, the required federal sex ed states that "Material must not promote contraception and/or condom use (as opposed to risk elimination). A curriculum must not promote or encourage sexual activity outside of marriage. A curriculum must not promote or encourage the use of any type of contraceptives outside of marriage or refer to abstinence as a form of contraception."

Additionally, "The curriculum must have a clear message regarding the importance of student abstinence from sexual activity until marriage and must emphasize that the best life outcomes are more likely obtained if an individual abstains until marriage. Throughout the entire curriculum, the term 'marriage' must be defined as 'only a legal union between one man and one woman as a husband and wife,' and the word 'spouse' refers only to a person of the opposite sex who is a husband or a wife. (Consistent with federal law.) The curriculum must teach the psychological and physical benefits of sexual abstinence-until-marriage for youth. Information on contraceptives, if included, must be age-appropriate and presented only as it supports the abstinence message being presented. Curriculum must not promote or endorse, distribute or demonstrate the use of contraception or instruct students in contraceptive usage."

That sure goes a long way toward the real questions kids have about sex. The United States has the highest rate of teen pregnancy in the developed world, and American adolescents are contracting HIV faster than almost any other demographic group.

Texas, with all those great abstinence-only textbooks, has the highest rate of teen births in the nation. And, duh—abortion rates are lowest in states where teens have access to accurate contraception information. In April 2007, a twenty-page Columbia University study exposed that abstinence curriculum statements about condom use are medically inaccurate. The American Civil Liberties Union, tired of the Department of Health and Human Services ignoring repeated warnings about incorrect data, sent the department a letter threatening legal action. The ACLU is currently trying to get the DHHS to stop disseminating incorrect information—because doing so violates federal law.

Wow, the U.S. government violating its own federal law? Barack, Michelle, your iPhones are ringing. Again. It's some kid who wants to know if she's going to get AIDS because her boyfriend came on her leg. Before that, she said they just let it soak so it should be all right. Should I take a message? Have an intern call her later?

Contrast our sex-ed failures to Australia, where, according to Carmody, the new brand of teen sex ed is "really about what they're doing because a lot of programs tend to focus just on biology and safe sex, but they don't. They don't tell us how to work out how to do consent, how to communicate with people. Those sort of things were what they were interested in." As part of her sex-ed curriculum, the students did role-play (not that kind of role-play), learned how to interpret body language, practiced asserting themselves, and were coached to think about their sexual behaviors and expectations.

The Obamas represent change that most of us are hungry for, and in some cases, desperate for. So, here's how Barack can put an end to the war on public school sex education and the sharing of accurate sex information to people of all ages:

1) Kill the abstinence programs. Period. Think of them as creationism in schools: optional to include in curricula but privately funded only. Fire the f— out of anyone with a religious agenda in a position of power in relation to public health. We are a nation of many faiths—most of which are not being served with this nonsense.

2) My best friend's daughter is five, and brags that she has a boyfriend. Craft programs that are age appropriate so kids understand what they're doing every step of the way. Take a cue from England, where the Sex and Relationship Education program centers on "All About Us: Living and Growing" videos for five- to seven-year-olds, seven- to nine-year-olds and nine- to eleven-year-olds, with workbooks about healthy sexual relationships for kids (and adults) with learning disabilities.

3) Require all sex-ed programs to include practical information about reproduction (including a woman's right to choose and male responsibilities of parenthood), contraception, STDs and STIs, sexual pleasure, masturbation, consent, homosexuality, sexual tolerance, and gender identity. Kids are dealing with all this stuff; adults need to stop lying to themselves and have honest discourse with kids about it.

4) Set aside federal funding for a teen sex-ed counselor to be on school staff at all times, exclusively for hotline-style accurate sex information, and completely confidential. Our kids' health and futures depend on it. Require that they are tech- and Internet-savvy.

5) Create a task force to research and implement outreach programs that visit schools for presentations on relevant and current sexual issues. This could include the Gardasil vaccination (HPV shot), presentations on transgender issues, workshops on sexual consent, rape prevention and self-defense for girls, age-

appropriate sex-ed books, religious faith and sexuality, and sexual questions around—yes—political scandals.

Michelle, Barack—I think you're cool, and you might just totally get what young girls and boys are going through. Or at least I want to think that. We need this change more than ever.

July 2008

How old were you the first time you had sex?

If you were a teenager when you "lost it," did you do it because you wanted social status or peer acceptance? For love? Was it your idea, or against your wishes? Or—did you try it because you thought it might just feel really good? Like, you know, warm apple pie?

Chances are good that if you had first-time sex under the age of consent, it wasn't for reproductive reasons—though it's a typical unintended consequence. Ask Bristol Palin. With your hormones in teenage overdrive and senses reeling, it's likely it was the pleasure principle, and not moral family factors, that had you dropping trou before you were barely legal.

Last week, Britain's new sexual health booklet hit the press, causing a furor by telling health-care practitioners who work with kids/teens that pleasure is an important principle in overall sexual health. The pamphlet was not distributed to adolescents but to adults who teach sexuality to kids: the underlying message of the booklet was to encourage "sexual awareness" in kids and that "sex is something that is meant to be enjoyed." It also explicitly encouraged young people to delay losing virginity until they were sure they would enjoy the experience. AP reported:

LONDON (AP) -- Britain's National Health Service has a message for teens: Sex can be fun.

Health officials are trying to change the tone of sex education by urging teachers to emphasize that sexual relations can be healthy and pleasurable instead of simply explaining the mechanics of sex and warning about diseases.

The new pamphlet, called "Pleasure," has sparked some opposition from those who believe it encourages promiscuity among teens in a country that already has high rates of teenage pregnancy and sexually transmitted diseases.

The National Health Service in the city of Sheffield produced the booklet, which has a section called "an orgasm a day" that encourages educators to tell teens about the positive physical and emotional effects of sex and masturbation, which is described as an easy way for people to explore their bodies and feel good. Like more traditional sex education guides, it encourages demonstrations about how to use condoms and other contraceptives.

Some professionals have hailed the new approach as a welcome antidote to traditional sex education, which they say can be long on biological facts but short on information about the complexity of human relationships. (...)

Predictably, some American conservatives reacted to the U.K.'s simple but revolutionary booklet with panties in a firm bunch, saying that such an attitude will "encourage promiscuity." Which is pretty much what we can predict them to say because they're so sexually repressed they still actually believe in dated moral-religious shame-drenched notions like "promiscuity." The argument seems to be that encouraging enjoyment of healthy masturbation to a teen will suddenly mean the kid will lose control and no longer know the difference between right and wrong and go on a sex spree of some kind. Tell them it's okay to explore and look out! We'll have skyrocketing teen pregnancy and teen STD rates—oh, wait. Eight years of abstinence education, and a sharp rise in these rates thanks to Bush (according to the CDC) have produced precisely that.

So much for the "hands off" approach. Talk about not understanding human social dynamics, let alone teen social dynamics. In my opinion, the conservative backlash just shows me that America's anti-sex, anti-pleasure pundits are the ones who will enact their greatest fears and lose their f---ing minds should they give in to a single moment of pleasure. They don't have the decision-making skills to know what's appropriate and safe, and what's not—because they've denied this type of understanding and exploration of sex's pleasure principles from everyone else for so long.

We're two hundred+ days into Obama's shift, and while we're waiting for all that change, the current state of sex ed in America is a flattened, empty, deserted war zone of sexlessness—at least Obama did eliminate federal abstinence education program funding from the 2010 budget.

After eight long years of abstinence education's war against sex information, we could do with more than a little of the U.K.'s harm-reduction approach to teaching kids about sexual pleasure—because teens are going to be having sex no matter what you tell them. I was discussing the new booklet with a friend who grew up in London and got a simple retort, "That's because we don't have religion in our government like you do." Say what you want about the separation of church and state, but the writing's been on the bathroom wall for a long time. And it doesn't say, "For a good time, call the Bush twins." Okay, maybe it does.

America not only needs to admit that teens have sex, but that they really like doing it—so they do it more than once. Unless you're 'lucky' it's actually not easy to get pregnant: you have to time it right with a fertile partner, and do it right, to fertilize an egg. And it's not a matter of imagining that sex will feel good that encourages repetition; otherwise teens wouldn't be trying it and trying it, again and again.

We can't educate kids about sex and give them tools to make the right choices for themselves, their families, their morals and beliefs and their communities unless we allow them the benefit of the doubt that they can handle the fact that sex feels good. That sex is healthy and should be pleasure-filled at whatever stage of development is right for them—and if they're old enough to ask, they're old enough to deserve an honest answer. When they're deprived of the feel-good truth, that's when kids (and adults) lose the ability to create tools to help them self-individuate their own healthy sexuality.

Rebuilding America's sex ed will result in a healthier country. Right now, in public schools across the nation it's a crapshoot as to what kids are being taught: in some places kids get abstinence sermons, in a few others they receive medical information about reproduction, and in even fewer they get some social counseling—with the genders neatly separated, of course. We need to teach teens about sex in a three-pronged approach: scientific (reproduction and STD/STI information), social (behaviors, appropriateness, communication and permission), and pleasure (feeling good about themselves, becoming aware of their own bodies so that when they do have sex it is healthy and feels good).

But according to conservative adults, this is just going to encourage promiscuity: "loose morals" and indiscriminate sexual choices. Good thing kids these days have the Internet.

The sex-ed revolution will not be televised. It's already on YouTube.

July 2009

A Cunning Linguist
John Thursday

How fondly I recall my ménages à trois: the quiet conspiracy, the jealous glances, Dusty Springfield on the stereo.

Yet, I have never had a ménage à trois, for ménages à trois have been rechristened. One night, when no one was looking, they became three-ways.

Some fool stole a hyphen, added a number and voilà, a house of three became a conference call, romance became business.

It may seem like a small thing, but for such a physical pleasure, our sexual delights are all about language.

A ménage à trois is something that takes place in a pied-à-terre. A three-way takes place in your cousin Steve's living room.

Indulge me in some examples.

Diddling a dame is completely different from balling a babe.

You lay a lady, but you do a chippy.

It's easy to finger-fuck a floozy but you had better bang a broad.

I, myself, have gotten dirty with damsels.

I've been randy with Rapunzel, raunchy with Cinderella, and used the whole fist on Thumbelina.

The back of a trollop in a back alley differs from the front of a strumpet in back of the bar.

You can spank a skank or snog a bird, but snogging a skank will leave you quite rank.

I've spent money on a honey but only taken home a doll.

I've gone all the way with a betty and fallen in love with a stone fox.

I've suckled a breast and thrilled to see boobs—but I've only cum on a pair of tits.

I've pinched a tush and slapped a bottom—but I've only fucked an ass.

It's anal sex if she went to college. Butt sex if she didn't. And get-the-hell-out-of-there! if she's Presbyterian.

If the word is wrong, all is lost.

Ever been topped by a pushy bottom leaving you bottomed while on top?

Howard Stern once got in trouble over a conversation he had on the air concerning an act he called a "blumpkin."

The only word I've ever heard for an act combining oral sex with a bowel movement is "blumper."

So, if there's no such thing as a blumpkin, should Howard Stern get in trouble?

The word is the thing.

A blumpkin sounds like something a hobbit eats at Christmas while a blumper, well, that's just dirty, filthy; in fact, it's worthy of a skank.

Felching sounds like an act not for the faint of heart. It's a word well suited to encompass an ass, a straw, and an orgasm.

What would nineteen-year-olds look forward to learning if not for words like *felching*?

Queef is a wonderful little word: only cooters and pussies queef.

A cunt farts.

And a vagina pretends nothing happened.

In the same way, only a penis can be flaccid.

A dick is soft.

A prick is regrouping.

And a cock pretends it never happens.

In the beginning spooge and smegma are wonderful things, things we look forward to, moist onomatopoeias of a job well done.

But then, like a couple who doesn't know when to leave, they stick around; falling into crevices they will later ooze out from. Spooge and smegma, the evil twins of post-coitus.

Who coined these terms? We'll never know. But these unsung heroes have provided us with a quick and easy way to describe our sexual world.

Not all these words are in daily use, (my spell-check barely recognized any of them), but they are there for the taking as a way to enrich our experience. Which brings me back to the lout who stole my hyphen.

You cannot own the act until you own the word.

I did not have a three-way.

We did not make triangles of ourselves. There was no geometry, no directional signals.

A three-way is something you boast about. It is a phrase without grace, a phrase reflecting the numbers, not the experience. There is nowhere to go from a three-way. The story has been told, you've jumped to the end, and you've climaxed too soon.

A ménage à trois is a memory to keep you warm on a lonely night.

A ménage à trois, a house of three, only sets the scene. There's the feel of sex, there's the house, and there are the three people.

It begs the question, "What was the house like?"

Once I had a ménage à trois with a doll and a dame. Another time it was with a betty and a fox.

There were no blumpers or felching involved.

In the beginning there were breasts and bottoms, but by the end it was all tits and ass.

Vaginas were perfumed, pussies queefed, and in the end I was very, very flaccid.

SWL(actating)F Seeking Sex with No Strings Attached
Rachel Sarah

On Thanksgiving Day my boyfriend walked out the door. Our daughter was seven months old, and I'll never know for sure what put him over the edge. He was bipolar. He drank. He was fragile. He didn't leave a forwarding address.

This was a time when I believed that love would overcome anything. Well, it certainly overcame me. The very first thing I did, even before crying, was to sit down on the living room rug and nurse my daughter, Mae. Nursing was my landing pad. It was the place where my milk could turn my anger into white, warm calmness. Nursing had the same soothing effect on my baby, no matter how hungry, agitated, red-faced, and cranky she was at the start. Nothing beat nursing.

No matter how alone I felt, those times that Mae lay on my chest, her tiny hands kneading my breasts, milk flowing from me, I knew that I could do this alone. Not only did nursing nourish

Mae, it nourished me. But it wasn't long after her father split town—as Mae's first birthday approached without a sign from him, I knew he wasn't coming back—that friends started to ask me, "When are you going to get back out there?"

As in *date*? They had to be kidding. Not only was I a twenty-nine-year-old single mom with dishes in the sink and baby clothes with stains I'd never actually scrub out, but I breastfed "on demand." How in the world could I even think about hooking up with some hot man when my cha-chas were making milk?

"But look at you!" my girlfriends (who were all married) said to me. "You're attractive, and you're young."

Maybe they were right. About getting back out there, anyway. As the months passed, I started to notice men: our building manager—who gave Mae stuffed animals and called her "Little Guacamole"— and the UPS man, who rolled his packages past me.

Still, noticing men in the hallway was *not* the same as dating them. I'm grateful that back then I did not sit down at my computer and type *lactating and dating* into Google. If I had, I *never* would have gone on a date. Because recently, while writing this essay, I turned to my computer to do some research, in hopes of finding a thoughtful example of what it means to balance these two acts. I hoped to come across a first-person essay in *Redbook* about a mother's deep feelings, something to inspire me as I worked.

One of the first things that came up, however, was a site called MilkMyTits.com. Men were looking for "mature women willing to breastfeed me."

Gross. I kept scrolling through the sites that Google brought up; there *had* to be something. But they were all the same: white men in their forties in search of sweet breast milk. My breasts had always been one of the most sensual parts of me. Before motherhood, when a man put his lips around my nipple, it made my body rain—not a light sprinkle, either. If I slept with a man as a nursing mom, my breasts would rain on him. Perhaps, after undressing, I could open my closet, pull out an umbrella, and hand it to him: "You might need this...."

I couldn't remember if I'd slept with Mae's father in the weeks before he'd left for good. If I had, I didn't remember the details. He was shut down and hungover; I was absorbed with my baby. I lived in the world of womanhood for years, and now I was a mother. But who says that you can't live in both worlds? Some mothers I knew wore bras to bed because they didn't want to leak on the mattress—or their husbands. That's how they divided their realms. But I wanted to be a woman who lived in both worlds; I wanted to be the kind of woman who didn't care if she spurted.

One of my best friends in New York City told me that she wanted to set me up on a blind date. Ironically, she was the same friend who, in 2002, was thrown out of the public library in Manhattan for breastfeeding her daughter. She'd been nursing in an empty reading room, when a female security guard screamed at her to "Take that outside." The guard didn't know that my friend, Susan Light, was a lawyer who took it straight to the media, after which the library expressed "deep regret" over the incident and immediately sent a memo to remind staff of the right of women to breastfeed.

"I want to date, but I can't," I told my friend.

"Why not?"

"I'm nursing."

"So?" she said.

"What would I wear?" I huffed. "A nursing bra?"

She laughed.

"No, really," I said. "I'd have to bring my pump along, for after my drink."

Little did my mother-friend know that the blind date she wanted to set me up with might have had a breastfeeding fetish. She told me that he was a lawyer, too, "a cute one." After chatting on the phone with the lawyer—his call woke me as I fell asleep while nursing Mae in the bed we share—I decided to go for it. I've always considered myself to be open-minded about anything intimate. Maybe I was rebelling against my Catholic mother, but I certainly was not a prude. I decided that I'd keep the date short and sweet—and I'd nurse before leaving so (I hoped) I wouldn't leak.

The following Friday, after enlisting another girlfriend to babysit, I dashed out the door to meet the lawyer at a bar. When I got inside, he waved. I didn't see the cuteness—he had a receding hairline—but maybe I was too nervous.

Still, he did the right thing: he asked if I had a photo of Mae, and when I pulled one from my wallet, he used the word *adorable*.

"She is," I said. "I'm late because I was nursing her before bed—"

"You were nursing her?"

That's when I noticed the sparkle in his eyes. Maybe I'd misread? But no.

"A woman who's lactating!" he said, way too loudly. "What a turn-on!"

I waited for the punch line, but he was not joking. I've always had this untactful knack for blurting out details that shock people—I do it without thinking. Why did I tell him that I was breastfeeding? Nursing was such an essential part of who I was, it was like telling someone, "The sitter was running late, I'm sorry—"

It's always *after* the fact when I realize I should be wearing a soft muzzle. The lawyer's enthusiasm was a sure giveaway that I'd said too much. I didn't know if I should crawl under the table or give him a high-five. Was I flattered or freaked out? Or a little of both?

But the truth was, if any possible romantic date of mine was squeamish about the fact that I was breastfeeding, I did need to know this up front. I mean, if I hadn't said anything, and then all of a sudden he looked down and noticed the wet spots on my blouse, that would have been interesting.

And that's exactly what happened.

If you've ever breastfed, you know that just thinking about nursing can, well, have certain consequences. My breasts were flooding with milk. I had no control over it, and when I looked down, there was a damp spot on my chest.

Maybe it was all in the name of discovery, but perhaps more important, I liked the fact that this man acknowledged who I was: a woman *as well as* a nursing mother. He could have overlooked that wet spot on my blouse. He could have glanced at his watch, embarrassed, and said, "I'd better get home."

At the time I wasn't interested in having him—or anyone, for that matter—as a companion. I was an unseasoned single mom who was trying to get over her ex. I was still trying to get a handle on raising my daughter solo. I wasn't ready for a relationship. But I *did* crave sex. And I was curious. I wanted to know what it felt like to have a man drink my milk.

Afterward, when I told a couple of friends what had happened, they scrunched their noses up. "You let him do *what?*"

Much to the dismay of my girlfriend who was babysitting, I brought him home. As my daughter slept in the other room, I let him unbutton my blouse and run his mouth across the edge of my bra. I let him touch me. When I started to leak, he was ecstatic. He told me that he'd never tasted anything so sweet in his life. (Yes, I wondered if, maybe, his mother had never breastfed him.) But this is what mattered most: he wanted me as I was, and I didn't have to hide any of it.

Toward a Performance Model of Sex
Thomas MacAulay Millar

Sally has a problem. Sally is a music slut. She plays with everyone. She has two regular bands, and some sidemen she jams with. When parties get late and loud, she will pull out her instrument and play with people she just met, people she hardly knows, people whose names she cannot remember—or never knew! She plays for money, she plays for beer, sometimes she even plays just to get an audience, because she likes the attention.

This paragraph makes no sense, at least not when taken literally, but the adoption of the concept of "slut" is so clear that the paragraph is, on even the most casual read, a thinly veiled metaphor for sex. The reason it makes no literal sense is that playing music does not share essential characteristics with the way Western culture models sex.

Rape is an act of war against women, one that can be committed only because of an entire culture of support, which makes most rapes permissible. Not all of the structures of rape support are about sexual culture: racism, classism, and the prison-industrial complex, as just a few examples, create circumstances under which some women can be and are raped with impunity. So simply changing the cultural model for sex will not undermine the social support for all kinds of rape. But many rapists acquire what is sometimes called a "social license to operate"[1] from the model of sex as a commodity (which constructs consent as the "absence of no") and from its close corollary, the social construct of "slut."

Without the notion of the slut, many rapists lose their license to operate—the notion exists only within a model of sex that analogizes it to property or, more specifically, to a commodity. The "commodity model" should be displaced by a model of sex as performance, which sits better with the notions of enthusiastic participation (or the "presence of yes," as distinct from the "absence of no") that many feminists argue for.[2]

We live in a culture where sex is not so much an act as a thing: a substance that can be given, bought, sold, or stolen, that has a value and a supply-and-demand curve. In this "commodity model," sex is like a ticket; women have it and men try to get it. Women may give it away or may trade it for something valuable, but either way it's a transaction. This puts women in the position of not only seller, but also guardian or gatekeeper—of what Zuzu

---

[1] The term was coined in extractive industries in response to environmental and other stakeholder criticisms.

[2] Among those who have eloquently described consent as "enthusiastic participation" is feminist author and blogger Amanda Marcotte. The author and Ms. Marcotte discussed these ideas at some length on one of the earlier feminist blogs, Alas! A Blog, in 2005. In her book *It's a Jungle Out There* (Seal Press, 2008) and on her blog, Pandagon, as well as in comments on other feminist blogs, she has expanded on these ideas and referred to a "conquest model" of sex, a concept that is both related to and distinct from the approach in this essay, which first appeared in comments at Feministing, the blog founded by editor Jessica Valenti. Ms. Marcotte's thinking and the views expressed here are closely related but have evolved independently.

of Shakesville, a feminist blog,³ refers to as the "pussy oversoul": women are guardians of the tickets; men apply for access to them. This model pervades casual conversation about sex: women "give it up," men "get some."

The commodity model is shared by both the libertines and the prudes of our patriarchy. To the libertine, guys want to maximize their take of tickets. The prudes want women to keep the tickets to buy something really "important": the spouse, provider, protector.

The Abstinence Movement: Protecting the Asset

Purity balls and the chastity movement have provided countless opportunities for feminist mockery and outrage. This movement, most popular among Protestant evangelicals, has for several years found its way into our public school curricula through federally funded "abstinence-only education." Much of this movement can be summarized by the familiar old saying that men will not buy the cow when they can get the milk for free. That also summarizes the analysis: women are livestock, valued for what they provide, not as partners. Their produce is milk, which is taken, bottled, and sold. Milk is fungible. When we drink milk, we care about its quality, but not about the identity of the cow. We may appreciate the milk, but this does not extend to appreciation of the cow.⁴

The chastity movement is a practical set of principles, a set

---

3 Shakesville, http://shakespearssister.blogspot.com/.
4 The milk/cow analogy, though familiar, is an inexact way of describing the commodity model. It is also worth noting that the commodity model itself demonstrates a significant gain for the feminist movement. Not long ago in the history of European civilizations, marriage was a different kind of property transaction. The woman herself was property, exchanged between her father and her husband. Now, even in the most regressive elements of American culture, the discourse pays lip service to the notion that the woman is not herself property, but instead possesses property (sex), which the patriarchy proceeds to tell her how to make the best use of.

of investor's guidelines for maximizing the benefit of the commodity. Abstinence-only programs are quite blunt about this. One program advertised its 2007 conference with a logo of a diamond wrapped in a padlocked chain. The logo read, "Guard Your Diamond, Save Sex for Marriage for a Brighter Future!"[5] The diamond is the hymen, but (with the explicit reference to marriage) also the engagement ring—and the program wants young women to preserve the commodity to make this optimal trade.

This view, not incidentally, makes sense only if the property is not a fully renewable resource. A cow keeps giving milk. But the abstinence proponents tell us that a woman's commodity is not as valuable later as it will be when she first offers it: like olive oil, the "extra virgin" is worth a lot more, and the stuff from the later pressings is of an inferior grade. One Peoria, Illinois, purity ball volunteer said, "Girls have a wonderful gift to give, and we don't want them to give all of themselves away. What we want them to do is present themselves as a rose to their husband with no blemishes."[6]

The abstinence proponents are quite explicit about this also. They have a model for sluthood: a woman whose commodity is used up and worn out, whose commodity nobody would want except as a cheap alternative at a low price. This model is often taught with an eye toward making the metaphor as disgusting as possible. One program uses a piece of tape covered with arm hair after being stuck to and torn off of several students' forearms, and which is

---

[5] UltraTeenChoice.org. Another program, WAIT, lists "financial support" as one of the five needs of women. "The Content of Federally Funded Abstinence-Only Education Programs," United States House of Representatives Committee on Government Reform, Minority Staff Special Investigations Division, December 2004 (Waxman Report), pp. 17 and n. 79. Still another lauds the practice of bride-prices because they tell the bride she is "valuable to the groom and he is willing to give something valuable to her." Waxman Report, p. 17 and n. 82.
[6] Dahleen Glanton, "At Purity Dances, Virgin Belles Ring for Abstinence," *Chicago Tribune*, December 2, 2007.

then thrown in the trash.[7] Another has students pass an unwrapped Peppermint Patty around the entire class. A Nevada program actually aired a public service announcement that said girls would feel "dirty and cheap" after breaking up with a sex partner.[8]

The people who encourage young women to treat their virginity as precious property do not see themselves as anti-woman, though feminists generally do. They are so invested in the commodity framework that, from their perspective, trading the commodity for the best possible gain is the best outcome a woman could hope for. To that way of thinking, sex can only ever be transacted, and the transaction that is the most advantageous is the one that uses the highly valuable early product to maximum advantage, to secure the best possible marriage: a lifetime commitment to financial support, and hopefully even an attractive and chivalrous sex partner. If sex really were a commodity that degraded with repeated harvesting, that would be all that was possible. The abstinence proponents, at least those of them who genuinely buy their line, think they are telling women what is in their best interest, because a better world is beyond their grasp.

The Libertines: Acquiring the Commodity

On the spectrum of patriarchy, the religious conservatives of the abstinence movement stand at one end. At the other end are Joe Francis and his *Girls Gone Wild* empire, and all of the other cultural forces that see sex as property, but simply want women to permit men to exploit it more freely.[9]

This is clear from the internal dialogue among self-styled

---

7 Jay Parsons, "Sex Lady's lesson: Save yourself," *Denton Record-Chronicle,* March 30, 2007.
8 www.siecus.org/policy/egregrious_uses.pdf
9 "Libertines" is not an evocative term, and in fact insults a late and lamented East London punk band. A term more in keeping with the conception would be "poontang miners," reflecting puerile slang, misogyny, and unsustainable exploitation in one fell swoop.

"pickup artists," who attempt to procure sex partners using "game" techniques.[10] One moderator at an online pickup artist forum wrote, "Really improved my game and what girls will do for me. If I can get them folding all my laundry a day after they met me, think what I'll have them doing when they've been having a continuous orgasm for the past 15 minutes."[11] The writer makes it his goal to "get" the most out of women, in the form of either sex or labor.[12] (That commenter made the transition from household labor to sexual services without apparent irony. If service and commodity are not exactly congruent, they are certainly close cousins.)

Further, buying into the commodity model also means buying into its internal valuation method: that value derives from scarcity, so that any woman who expresses her sexuality by actually having sex partners is devalued. One poster wrote:

Recently, as soon as I hook up with a girl, I start to resent her, because it was SO easy to seduce her. My skills have gotten pretty good, and I've seduced two girls this past week, and immediately after it happened, I wasn't attracted to them anymore. I feel like, how can she be a high-value female if she was THAT easy to get in to bed.[13]

A forum moderator responded, "Too bad she's still a depreciating and often damaged asset."[14]

---

10 See generally, Neill Strauss, *The Game: Penetrating the Secret Society of Pickup Artists* (New York: HarperCollins, 2005).
11 Pick-up-artist-forum.com post entitled, "How Can I Release Her Inner Whore," Rye Lee comment, November 8, 2007, 5:08 AM, www.pick-up-artist-forum.com/how-can-i-release-her-inner-whore-vt10548.html.
12 In discussion of the commodity model, it is glaringly apparent that there is room for Marxist analysis of sex as work; while that analysis might be fruitful and even fascinating, it is beyond both the scope of the essay and the writer's expertise.
13 Pick-up-artist-forum.com post entitled "Fundamental Problem With Being a PUA," GravesRR7 comment, November 17, 2007, 12:56 AM, www.pick-up-artist-forum.com/fundamental-problem-with-being-a-pua-vt11181.html.
14 Starbuck on November 17, 2007, 3:32 PM.

These men openly adopt the commodity model as conducive to male privilege, because a better world is not in their perceived self-interest.

Nice Guys™: Applying for Access to the Pussy Oversoul

The term "Nice Guys™" has evolved in the feminist blogosphere to refer to passive-aggressive hetero men who complain that they are refused sex in favor of other men when, apparently, they deem themselves deserving. Usually, their belief system involves the idea that other men, who treat women badly, are much more appealing to women, and that they themselves are disadvantaged in a sexual marketplace by their refusal to abuse or trick women in certain ways. Their entire worldview depends on the commodity model, and on a corollary view of their own entitlement: that there must be some "proper" way for them to act and "get" sex; that if they do all the "right" things, they will unlock the lock and get laid. By contrast, do musicians really think that if they just do the right things, someone must form a band with them?

The combination of passive-aggressiveness, entitlement, and the certainty that sex is a commodity leads the Nice Guy™ to argue, in all seriousness, that rape is caused because Nice Guys™ seek sex but are rejected, and rape is their reaction to unfair rejection. A paradigmatic example of this argument appeared in a mammoth discussion of rape in a thread entitled "Some Guys Are Assholes But It's Still Your Fault If You Get Raped" at Alas! A Blog on June 15, 2005. Commenter Aegis posted this argument, which neatly encapsulates Nice Guy™ thinking:

Rape. As far as I understand, some of the times a man rapes a woman, it is after she has already rebuffed his advances. Male confusion about how to seek sex will obviously contribute to those males being rebuffed. Hence, male confusion about how to seek sex contributes to situations where rape is more likely to happen. In short, imagine a situation in which a proto-rapist becomes an actual date rapist because he didn't know how to induce the woman to be interested in having sex with him; if he had succeeded in doing so, she would have consented, and the situation where he decided to rape her would never have occurred.[15]

Aegis thus conceives of rape as the result of a man's frustration when he is refused something (the commodity) that he would be granted if he submitted a proper application for it. There is a term for something that is meant to be granted upon proper request: entitlement. To the Nice Guy™ way of thinking, the commodity is an entitlement: women are gatekeepers to the Pussy Oversoul, and should grant access upon proper application; or, more crudely, women are pussy vending machines.[16]

If only the Nice Guy™ were unique in this sense of entitlement! Rather, the Nice Guy™ expresses clearly the undercurrent of entitlement that runs through the culture. Men generally are constructed as the pursuers of sex, and taught that their proper pursuit will be rewarded. What straight men really need to learn is that women are humans, too, who get to make their own decisions about whether and with whom to have sex; and that nobody owes anyone sex.

Aegis lays out an argument that this entitlement leads to rape, but the path from rejection and disappointment to rape does not depend on misunderstanding, as Aegis believed. Instead, entitled men who believe that sex is a commodity and that they have been denied it wrongfully see rape as repossession. It belongs to them, and they resentfully use any tactic necessary to get it. These men see themselves as being in the same position as a man who

---

15 Aegis on June 34, 2005, 12:08 PM.
16 Amanda Marcotte's term, in *It's a Jungle Out There* (Seal Press, 2008), which evolved from the author's "sex vending machines" in the Feministing thread that was the original source for this essay.

finds that his stolen car is in the custody of a garage: he may not know whether the garage stole it or found it, but it is his, and he is entitled to get it back. If they refuse to give it up after he asks the right way, he will lie to them, trick them, or threaten them if necessary to get it. He can write a check and stop payment; he can just get in and drive off. Because it is his car, it is his right. When these men apply that thinking to sex, it's as if the woman standing between them and the pussy is an irrelevance, a hindrance.

The Problems of the Commodity Model
The commodity model has a number of problems. Principally, it reinforces patriarchal sex roles and constructs, and it allows for the construction of the concept of sluthood, which is key to at least one family of rape-supportive ideas.

The commodity model is inherently heteronormative and phallocentric. If two men have sex, who is the supplier and who is the demander? The commodity model requires one person to "give it up" and the other to want to "get some," the "it" and "some" being the paradigmatic commodity: crudely, pussy. When nobody in the equation has an actual vagina, the model either imposes a notion of one or presupposes unlimited consumption. So, for example, thinking mired in this model may assume a "who's the girl" conception that penetrative sex always occurs and that femininity should be imputed to the enveloping partner. Separately but not unrelated is the long-standing slur that gay men are inherently and compulsively promiscuous, there being no gatekeeper to restrict the supply of the commodity. The commodity model doesn't deal any better with sex between two women—it simply imagines the economic problem in reverse, so that two gatekeepers reluctantly, if ever, "give it up."

The commodity model also functions as all-purpose rape

apology. The logical conclusion of this model is that rape is narrowly understood and consent is presumed. Under the commodity model, consent is not necessarily enthusiastic participation, or even necessarily an affirmative act. If someone tries to take something and the owner raises no objection, then that something is free for the taking. To this way of thinking, consent is the absence of "no." It is therefore economically rational to someone with this commodity concept of sex that it can be taken; rape is a property crime in that view. In the past, the crime was against the male owner of women (let's not sugarcoat it; until very recently, women were in a legal way very much male property, and still are in many places and ways). Even among more enlightened folks, if one takes a commodity view of sex, rape is still basically a property crime against the victim.

Some of the most common rape-apologist arguments follow from the commodity model. For example, rape apologists often echo Katie Roiphe's argument from her 1994 book, *The Morning After,* that women who have "bad" sex and later regret it interpret the experience as rape. In fact, the terminology of a transaction is often applied: "buyer's remorse." To that way of thinking, women have made a transaction that cannot be undone, and seek a form of refund by calling it nonconsensual after the fact. But it is fanciful to imagine a circumstance in which enthusiastic participation quickly turns not to regret, but to denial that consent existed at the time. This argument works only if consent is simply acquiescence, even grudging acquiescence. Because they cast sex as commodity, rape apologists can easily make the same caveat emptor arguments about sex that one makes in used-car sales: that a deal is a deal, however reluctantly, grudgingly, or desperately one side accepts it.

In fact, the commodity model is, at its core, an adversary model (though one might stop short of calling it a zero-sum game, except perhaps in the minds of the most open misogynists). The negotiation is not a creative process but a bargaining process, where each side seeks and makes concessions. Each side wants to get something that the other does not want to give.

What naturally arises from the commodity model is a tendency of property transactions: they are often not equally advantageous, and depend on bargaining power. Since some duress and coercion are common, in order for commerce to flourish it is necessary to have rules about when someone is stuck with the bargain they made, even if they regret it or never really liked it in the first place. This is what rape apologists do every time: defend the transaction by holding the unhappy participant responsible, emphasizing her agency, minimizing coercion, and insisting on the finality of bargains.

When applied to sex, every feminist knows what this looks like. Rape apologists argue that once consent is given it cannot be withdrawn; that acquiescence under the influence is consent; that women who do not clearly say no assume the risk.[17]

The Performance Model of Sex

Returning to Sally the musician, we do not believe some things to be true of her that the commodity model presumes about sex. The better model for sex is the one that fits the musician: a performance model, where sex is a performance, and partnered sex is a collaboration. Music is an obvious metaphor. (There are others: dance, which is also frequently a two-partner but sometimes a multipartner activity; or sports, which imports a problematic competitive aspect.)

---

[17] These discussions often unconsciously seem to recapitulate the development of law, particularly the law of the Gilded Age and pre-Depression era that heavily favored externalizing costs and risks to workers and consumers.

The commodity model assumes that when a woman has sex, she loses something of value. If she engages in too much sex, she will be left with nothing of value. It further assumes that sex earlier in her history is more valuable than sex later. If she has a lot of sex early on, what she has left will not be something people will esteem highly. But a musician's first halting notes at age thirteen in the basement are not something of particular value. Only an obsessive completist would want a recording of a young musician's practice before she knew what she was doing; and then only after that musician has made her mark by playing publicly, well, and often. She gets better by learning, by playing a lot, by playing with different people who are better than she is. She reaches the height of her powers in the prime of her life, as an experienced musician, confident in her style and conversant in her material. Her experience and proven talent are precisely why she is valued.

Because it centers on collaboration, a performance model better fits the conventional feminist wisdom that consent is not the absence of "no," but affirmative participation. Who picks up a guitar and jams with a bassist who just stands there? Who dances with a partner who is just standing and staring? In the absence of affirmative participation, there is no collaboration.

Like the commodity model, the performance model implies a negotiation, but not an unequal or adversarial one. The negotiation is the creative process of building something from a set of available elements. Musicians have to choose, explicitly or implicitly, what they are going to play: genre, song, key and interpretation. The palette available to them is their entire skill set—all the instruments they have and know how to play, their entire repertoire, their imagination and their skills—and the product will depend on the pieces each individual brings to the performance.

Two musicians steeped in Delta blues will produce very different music from one musician with a love for soul and funk and another with roots in hip-hop or 1980s hardcore. This process involves communication of likes and dislikes and preferences, not a series of proposals that meet with acceptance or rejection.

The performance model gives us room to expand comfortably beyond the hetero paradigm. This model encounters no conceptual problem when two men or two women or more than two people have sex. Their collaboration will produce a different performance because their histories and preferences differ, as do all people's, and the result is influenced (not constrained) by the bodies people have. The performance model even has better explanatory power than the commodity model in looking at a queer man and woman having sex. The commodity model does not differentiate this scenario from that of a hetero couple; the performance model predicts that this union will be different. To stretch a metaphor perhaps too far, the musicians come from different genres and will play music differently, even when they are writing it for the same arrangement of instruments.

A performance model is one that normalizes the intimate and interactive nature of sex. The commodity model easily divides sex into good and bad, based on the relative gains from the transaction, mapping closely to conservative Christian sexual mores. Under a performance model, the sexual interaction should be creative, positive, and respectful even in the most casual of circumstances, and without regard to what each partner seeks from it.

The performance model directly undermines the social construct of the slut. That is why the music-slut paragraph that begins the essay is so obviously a sex reference. There is no such thing as a music slut, and the concept makes sense only if it blatantly borrows the idea of slut from sex—an idea available to us because we are so used to talking and thinking about sex in a commodity model.

By centering collaboration and constructing consent as affirmative, the performance model also changes the model for rape. Forcing participation through coercion in a commodity model is a property crime, but in a performance model it is a disturbing and invasive crime of violence, a kind of kidnapping. Imagine someone forcing another, at gunpoint, to play music with him. It is perhaps a musical act (as rape has a sexual component, more central for some rapists than others), but there is no overlooking the coercion. The fact that it is musical would not in any way distract from the fact that it was forced, and sensible people might scratch our heads at how strange it is for someone to want to play music with an unwilling partner. Certainly, nobody would discount the coercion merely because the musician performing at gunpoint played music with other people, or even with the assailant before, which is an argument rape apologists make regularly when the subject is sex instead of music. B. B. King has played with everybody, but no one would argue that he asked for it if someone kidnapped him and made him cut a demo tape with a garage band of strangers.

Under a performance model of sex, looking for affirmative participation is built into the conception. Our children take their conceptions of sex from their parents first, and from the wider culture. If our boys learn from their preadolescence that sex is a performance where enthusiastic participation is normal and pressure is aberrant, then the idea that consent is affirmative, rather than the absence of objection, will be ingrained. In such an environment, many kinds of rape that are accepted, tolerated and routinely defended would lose their social license to operate.

The Client Voyeur
debauchette

I'm a voyeur. I like watching without being seen, and I find comfort in big cities and subways, places where I can feel anonymous. A few years ago, I was hired by a voyeur, a true voyeur, a fetishist. I was working as a role-play girl at the time, specializing in various forms of psychological domination, but this request was unusual. He wanted to watch a woman sit in a chair for a few hours, and nothing more—which, in itself, was an amazing idea, that a client could be satisfied by simply looking, but the thought of being watched so intensely made me uncomfortable. It was only after my agent pushed the issue that I reluctantly agreed. "Get a push-up bra," she said.

I dashed out for a quick lingerie run, browsing shops until I settled on a black satin bra so thickly padded that it felt more like a prosthetic than a garment. It was overkill, a defensive purchase, as though the padding could work as a protective barrier. And when

I dressed, I cloaked myself in the archetype of the sexy secretary, the tight skirt, the silk stockings, the mile-high heels, the ruby red lips. All role-play requires some illusion and fantasy, but I wanted to inflate the illusion to deflect his attention.

We met in his hotel room. He was a good-looking man in his forties, a media professional in town for a few meetings. After some small talk, he settled into the sofa. On the coffee table in front of him, he'd laid out a pack of cigarettes, a lighter, an ashtray, and a copy of the *New York Times*. There was the understanding that I'd keep to myself—no conversation, no eye contact. I was seated directly across from him in a single, straight-backed chair. After a pause, I started to fidget with nervous energy. I crossed and uncrossed my legs, dug through my purse, pulled out some gum, put it back, pulled out some reading material. I tried to avoid looking up, but in my restlessness, I snuck a quick peek. When I saw that he was hidden behind an open newspaper, I relaxed, lowered my eyes, settled into my chair, and began to read.

The experience was strange. At first, I felt very in control, fully embodying the persona of a secretary. I think my mannerisms must have been contrived and affected, but as time passed, I became aware of the silence. Every sound in the room caught my attention, the muffled noise from the street below, the sound of luggage being dragged down the hall of the hotel. I stopped thinking about how I looked and just listened while I tried to read. He lit a cigarette and inhaled deeply. I tucked a strand of hair behind my ear and turned the page.

Then I became aware of my body. I could feel myself breathe, and with it I could feel my blouse pull taut across my breasts with each inhale, the silk on silk of my stockings when I moved my legs. I was aware of my skin and its surface sensations, the places where I'm sensitive, the pressure of the bra digging into my ribs, the tightness of the skirt at my waist and hips. When I glanced up a second time, I caught him watching me, intensely, the way I would've watched him if we'd been strangers on the subway. And that's when it changed. It wasn't about two people reading in a room anymore. His attention was aggressive and focused, and I felt a kick of adrenaline and blushed, part surprise, part embarrassment. I wanted to turn away, but I just lowered my eyes and tried to slow the pounding in my chest. I tried to restore control and think like a role-play girl, but his attention was intimidating and exciting.

The entire room felt sexual. I could feel it in my chest, my thighs, my pussy. My skin. When I crossed my legs, the silk of my underwear pulled tight across my cunt. I felt like prey, which was exciting and unnerving. There were fight-or-flight butterflies in my gut for what felt like hours, but I kept my composure and stayed very still, and when the adrenaline subsided, I was aroused. I wanted something to happen; to undress, spread my legs, crawl on my hands and knees, lift my hips like a cat in heat. I wanted to be violated. I kept my eyes down and let my mind drift to images of raw, rough sex.

He whispered, "Stand up." Another surge of adrenaline. I stood up slowly.

I heard a slow drag on a cigarette, a slow exhale, and then he whispered again, "Undress."

I steadied my hands as I unbuttoned my blouse, excited by the thought of stripping. I reached behind and unzipped my skirt, shimmied out of its tightness, and stepped out of the material pooled at my feet.

"Stop there," he whispered. I wanted to keep going.

He approached me, but I kept my eyes averted, taking him in through my peripheral vision. He walked toward me and moved his hands near my waist, pausing for a moment before drawing them back, and the anticipation, the frustration was excruciating. I was breathing heavily as he walked around me, like I was some kind of freestanding sculpture, half stripped but very naked. My heart was pounding, and I was thinking, *Just touch me.* His attention and the restrained sexual energy had me desperate for physical contact.

The intensity reminded me what it felt like to want, and not have. He hadn't touched me, but in all the silence and focused attention, I'd slowly let go of my resistance, transformed from defensive affectation to open, raw lust. I don't know what it was that he found gratifying, whether it was the act of looking or my own slow unraveling to a state of eager submission, but after several long minutes, and several long, slow drags on his cigarette, he whispered, "Excuse me," and left the room.

I stood there, half naked, waiting, throbbing. I became aware of the silence again, the noise from the street, the movement in the hallway. He returned with a healthy tip, and with that, the session was over. I dressed awkwardly, thanked him, and left the hotel to step out into the noise of New York.

It was hours before my body was quiet again.

About the Authors

BRIAN ALEXANDER, guest judge for *Best Sex Writing 2009*, is the writer of MSNBC.com's "Sexploration" column, author of *America Unzipped: The Search for Sex and Satisfaction* (2008), and a frequent contributor to national magazines. He is also at work on another book. It has nothing to do with sex.

JESSE BERING is director of the Institute of Cognition and Culture at Queen's University Belfast in Northern Ireland, where he studies how the evolved human mind plays a part in various aspects of social behavior. He writes a weekly online column for *Scientific American* magazine called "Bering in Mind."

DAVID BLACK is a journalist, novelist, screenwriter and producer. His articles have been published in the *Atlantic*, the *New York Times Magazine*, *Harper's* and *Rolling Stone*. His novel *Like*

Father was named a notable book of the year by the *New York Times* and he received the Writers' Guild of America Award for *The Confession*.

VIOLET BLUE is the sex columnist for the *San Francisco Chronicle*, notorious blogger, high-profile tech personality, best-selling author and editor, podcaster, GETV reporter, technology futurist, public speaker (ETech, Google Inc.), sex-positive pundit in mainstream media (such as CNN and *Oprah* Magazine), and a Forbes Web Celeb. Find her at tinynibbles.com.

After spending years working on an arcane and socially irrelevant doctoral dissertation, DEBAUCHETTE dove into the world of sex work. She has worked as a nude model, a fetish worker, a call girl, and a courtesan, before retiring to work on the online magazine F/lthyGorgeousTh/ngs, which she cofounded with a fellow sex enthusiast.

JOHN DEVORE writes the "Mind of Man" column for The Frisky.com. A former *Maxim* Magazine editor, John has written for Comedycentral.com, Playboy.com, and for the infamous political parody Whitehouse.org. For two and a half years, he cohosted the radio show "DeVore and Diana" on Sirius Satellite Radio.

BETTY DODSON (dodsonandross.com) has been one of the principal voices for women's sexual pleasure and health for over three decades. Her books include the feminist classic *Liberating Masturbation: A Meditation on Selflove, Sex for One* and *Orgasms for Two*. In 1994, she earned a PhD in clinical sexology. She presented the first feminist slide show of vulvas at the 1973 NOW Sexuality Conference.

ABOUT THE AUTHORS

SETH MICHAEL DONSKY is a filmmaker whose work has screened at the Berlin, Seattle, London and Cinequest International Film Festivals and MoMA, New York. As a journalist he has been published in *Los Angeles Confidential*, *Gotham*, the *New York Press*, and the online versions of *ELLE Décor*, *Metropolitan Home* and *Home*. Contact sethmichaeldonsky.com.

ELLEN FRIEDRICHS lives in Brooklyn where she teaches health to middle and high school students. She also teaches human sexuality at Brooklyn College and runs the GLBT teens site for About.com. More of her writing can be found on her SexEdvice.com website and on the gURL.com State of Sex Education blog.

WILLIAM GEORGIADES worked in Manhattan media for over a decade, as the editor in chief of *BlackBook*, as the book reviews editor at the *New York Post*, as an assistant editor at *Esquire*, and as a contributor to *Vanity Fair*, *GQ*, the *Advocate* and the *London Times*, among others.

JOHANNA GOHMANN has written essays, articles and reviews for *Bust*, *Elle*, *Publisher's Weekly*, *Red*, Babble.com, the *Irish Independent* and others. A native of Indiana, she spent nine years in New York City writing about everything from werewolf erotica to the Queens Mineral Society. She currently resides in Dublin, Ireland.

CHRIS HALL is a bicoastal sex nerd who keeps one foot in San Francisco, one in New York, and his mind permanently in the gutter. Chris is cofounder of the website Sex in the Public Square (sexinthepublicsquare.org) and senior editor of Carnal Nation (carnalnation.com).

The author or coauthor of ten books about relationships and sexuality, JANET HARDY has traveled the world as a speaker and teacher on topics ranging from ethical multipartner relationships to erotic spanking and beyond.

DIANA JOSEPH (dianajoseph.net) is the author of *I'm Sorry You Feel That Way: The Astonishing but True Story of a Daughter, Sister, Slut, Wife, Mother and Friend to Man and Dog*.

PAUL KRASSNER (paulkrassner.com) is the founder, editor and frequent contributor to the free-thought magazine the *Realist*. He currently writes columns for *AVN Online* and *High Times*. His books include *In Praise of Indecency, Pot Stories for the Soul, Tales of Tongue Fu, One Hand Jerking* and *Confessions of a Raving Unconfined Nut*.

JUDITH LEVINE (judithlevine.com) is the author of four books, including *Harmful to Minors: The Perils of Protecting Children From Sex*, which won the 2002 *Los Angeles Times* book prize. She is an activist for women's freedom, civil liberties, and peace and currently serves as a director for the National Center for Reason & Justice and the American Civil Liberties Union's Vermont chapter.

THOMAS MACAULAY MILLAR is a New York-area litigator, a parent and spouse, a feminist, a progressive, a Scottish-American, and a cis-het-white male, not necessarily in that order. He contributes to *Yes Means Yes* Blog, Feministing Community, and sometimes Feministe.

"MICHELLE PERROT" is a pseudonym to protect her marriage.

She has published four books and her work has been featured in the *New York Times,* the *Washington Post* and *Brevity,* as well as other anthologies, magazines and journals. She lives with her family somewhere in the United States.

KIRK READ (kirkread.com) is a writer, performer, and event-maker based in San Francisco's Mission district. His books include *How I Learned to Snap* (American Library Association Honor), a memoir about being openly gay in a small Virginia high school, and *This is the Thing,* a collection of performance essays. He co-curates San Francisco's two longest-running queer open mics, Smack Dab and K'vetsh. He has toured the country twice with the Sex Workers' Art Show.

RACHEL SARAH is the author of *Single Mom Seeking: Play Dates, Blind Dates, and Other Dispatches from the Dating World* (Seal Press). When she's not contracting for Match.com, Rachel hosts a juicy blog at singlemomseeking.com for single moms and dads.

CHRISTINE SEIFERT is an associate professor of communication at Westminster College in Salt Lake City, Utah where she teaches professional writing and rhetoric. She earned a PhD in English from Oklahoma State University. Christine is currently working with an agent to revise her own young adult novel…sans vampires.

MONICA SHORES is an editor of and regular contributor to *Spread* magazine. She has also written for Alternet, the Rumpus, DCist, Popmatters, Boinkology and the *Feminist Review.* "Red Light Rights" is her biweekly column on CarnalNation.com.

RACHEL SWAN is a staff writer at the *East Bay Express* newspaper in Oakland, California.

JOHN THURSDAY is an erotic philosopher who has devoted his adult life to doing field research for his dissertation on Kant's lesser known work, *The Pure Critique of Fellatio*. In his down time he enjoys dancing, cooking and masturbating. You can find his work at Johnthursday.com.

MOLLENA WILLIAMS is a New York City born and raised writer, actress, solo-performer, BDSM Educator and Executive Pervert. She travels hither and yon speaking on a broad spectrum of subjects within the Leather Lifestyle. She's a founding member of the Crowded Fire Theater Company, lives in San Francisco and blogs at mollena.com.

About the Editor

RACHEL KRAMER BUSSEL (rachelkramerbussel.com) is a New York-based author, editor and blogger. She is the editor of *Best Sex Writing 2008* and *2009*, and has edited or coedited over twenty books of erotica, including *Peep Show, Bottoms Up: Spanking Good Stories; Spanked; Naughty Spanking Stories from A to Z 1* and *2; The Mile High Club; Do Not Disturb; Tasting Him; Tasting Her; Yes, Sir; Yes, Ma'am; He's on Top; She's on Top; Caught Looking; Hide and Seek; Crossdressing; Rubber Sex; Sex and Candy; Ultimate Undies; Glamour Girls* and *Bedding Down*. Her work has been published in over one hundred anthologies, including *Best American Erotica 2004* and *2006*, Zane's *Chocolate Flava 2* and *Purple Panties, Everything You Know About Sex Is Wrong, Single State of the Union* and *Desire: Women Write About Wanting*. She serves as senior editor at *Penthouse Variations*, and wrote the popular "Lusty Lady" column for the *Village Voice*.

Rachel has written for *AVN, Bust,* Cleansheets.com, *Cosmopolitan, Curve,* Fresh Yarn, TheFrisky.com, Gothamist, Huffington Post, Mediabistro, *Newsday, New York Post, Penthouse, Playgirl, Radar, San Francisco Chronicle, Tango, Time Out New York* and *Zink,* among others. She has appeared on "The Martha Stewart Show," "The Berman and Berman Show," NY1, and Showtime's "Family Business." She has hosted In the Flesh Erotic Reading Series since October 2005, which has featured everyone from Susie Bright to Zane, about which the *New York Times*'s UrbanEye newsletter said she "welcomes eroticism of all stripes, spots and textures." She blogs at lustylady.blogspot.com.

Check out the official *Best Sex Writing 2010* blog at bestsexwriting2010.wordpress.com and bestsexwriting.com for guidelines and more information about the series.

PERMISSIONS

"The Girl Who Only Sometimes Said No" by Diana Joseph was originally published in *I'm Sorry You Feel That Way: The Astonishing but True Story of a Daughter, Sister, Slut, Wife, Mother, and Friend to Man and Dog* (Putnam Adult, March 2009). "Secrets of the Phallus: Why Is the Penis Shaped Like That?" by Jesse Bering was originally published online at ScientificAmerican.com on April 27, 2009. "The Vagina Dialogues" by Johanna Gohmann was originally published in BUST, June/July 2009. "Sex Laws That Can Really Screw You" by Ellen Friedrichs was originally published at Alternet.org, June 12, 2009. "What Really Turns Men On" by John DeVore was originally published in a different form at TheFrisky.com. "It's a Shame About Ray" by Kirk Read was originally published in *Hos, Hookers, Call Girls, and Rent Boys: Professionals Writing on Life, Love, Money and Sex* edited by David Henry Sterry and R. J. Martin Jr. (Soft Skull Press, August 2009). "Remembering Pubic Hair" by Paul Krassner was originally published in *In Praise of Indecency: The Leading Investigative Satirist Sounds Off on Hypocrisy, Censorship and Free Expression* by Paul Krassner (Cleis Press, May 2009). "Sexual Outlaw" by Betty Dodson was originally published on Dodson's blog at dodsonandross.com. "Go Thin or Bust: How Berkeley's Mayer Laboratories Won the Battle of the Thin Condoms" by Rachel Swan was originally published in *East Bay Express,* November 19, 2008. "'Sex Surrogates' Put Personal Touch on Therapy" by Brian Alexander was originally published on MSNBC.com, March 26, 2009. "What's the Matter with Teens and Sexting?" is reprinted with permission from Judith Levine, "What's the Matter with Teen Sexting?," The American Prospect Online: February 02, 2009. www.prospect.org *The American Prospect,* 1710 Rhode Island Avenue NW, 12th Floor, Washington, DC 20036. All rights reserved. "Bite Me! (Or Don't)" by Christine Seifert was originally published in *Bitch,* Winter 2009 issue (No. 42). "Hot. Digital. Sexual. Underground" by David Black was originally published in *Playboy,* June 2009. "Lust and Lechery in Eight Pages: The Story of the Tijuana Bibles" by Chris Hall was originally published at Carnal Nation (carnalnation.com), March 20, 2009. "The Trouble with Safe Sex" by Seth Michael Donsky was originally published in *New York Press,* April 15-21, 2009. "The Future of Sex Ed" by Violet Blue was originally published as two separate pieces at Sfgate.com, the website of the *San Francisco Chronicle.* "A Cunning Linguist" by John Thursday was originally published in *Good Vibrations Magazine* (Goodvibes.com), January 7, 2009. "SWL(actating) F Seeks Sex with No Strings Attached," by Rachel Sarah, is excerpted from *Unbuttoned: Women Open Up About the Pleasures, Pains, and Politics of Breastfeeding,* edited by Dana Sullivan and Maureen Connolly. (c) 2009, used by permission from The Harvard Common Press. "Toward a Performance Model of Sex" by Thomas MacAulay Millar was originally published in *Yes Means Yes: Visions of Female Sexual Power and A World Without Rape,* edited by Jaclyn Friedman and Jessica Valenti (Seal Press, December 2008). "The Client Voyeur" by debauchette was originally published in F/lthyGorgeousTh/ngs (filthygorgeousthings.com), Issue One (May 2009). All other essays copyright 2010 by the individual authors.